MATIGARI

MATIGARI

❖

Ngũgĩ wa Thiong'o

❖

Translated from the Gĩkũyũ by
Wangũi wa Goro

AFRICA WORLD PRESS

Trenton | London | Cape Town | Nairobi | Addis Ababa | Asmara | Ibadan | New Delhi

AFRICA WORLD PRESS
541 West Ingham Avenue | Suite B
Trenton, New Jersey 08638

Copyright © Ngũgĩ wa Thiong'o, 1998
First AWP Edition, 1998

Cover Design by Linda Nickens
Book Design by Jonathan Gullery

This book is composed in Garamond and Stone Serif

Library of Congress Cataloging in Publication Data

Ngũgĩ wa Thiong'o, 1938-
   [Matigari. English]
   Matigari / Ngũgĩ wa Thiong'o : translated from the Gĩkũyũ by Wangũi wa Goro.
     p.   cm. -- (African writers library)
   Originally published: Oxford : Heinemann International, 1989.
   ISBN 0-86543-360-7
   I. Wangũi wa Goro. II. Title. III. Series.
PL8379.9.N4M3713   1996
896' .395432--dc21

                            96-44440
                              CIP

*This novel is dedicated to all those who love a good story;
and to all those who research and write on African orature;
and to all those committed to the development of literature
in the languages of all the African peoples.*

CONTENTS

A NOTE ON THE AMERICAN EDITION

I wrote *Matigari* in 1983-84 in a one-room apartment at Noel Road in Islington London. It was my second novel in the Gĩkũyũ language. It came out in Kenya in 1986. Since then the book itself has had a history almost rivaling that of the fictional story it carries within the hard covers.

The novel was written within my first three years of political exile from the Kenya I love. My writing the novel in Gĩkũyũ when there are hardly any significant speakers and readers of the language in Britain or abroad was my way of trying to cope with the harsh conditions of exile and to make a connection with Kenya. When the novel came out in October 1986, it was indeed received in the country very positively. People started talking about the main character, Matigari, as a real living person. He was after all asking questions, albeit in a fictional landscape, which many people in the country were asking. In a dictatorship, questions of truth and justice are paramount precisely because these two are the first to disappear in a such an environment. In the Kenya of 1986 and after, many intellectuals have been imprisoned, exiled, or killed for going about their literary and academic tasks of asking questions. So it is not surprising that the regime's internal spy network should have quickly heard of the exploits of this man Matigari who it seems was going about the country agitating the populace with endless questions about truth and justice. The dictator responded in character. He had the police issue a warrant for the arrest of Matigari. But the hardworking loyal policemen found out that the man they had come to arrest was only a fictional character in a book by the same title. The dictatorship reacted to this information by calling for the arrest of the book itself. And indeed, in a very well coordinated police action, they raided all the bookstores in the entire country sometime in February 1987 and took away all the copies of the novels, presumably to burn it or let it rot to death in a police garrison.

An English translation of the novel was then published in London in 1991. Here then was another irony. For a time the novel existed only in English and in exile abroad, thus sharing the fate of its author. Two years later copies of the book could be sold in the bookshops in Kenya; thus, in its English language form, the novel and the character could be read in Kenya, but not in its

Gĩkũyũ original. And it is only in 1997, under the new atmosphere of the struggle for multiparty democracy, that it was re-issued in its Gĩkũyũ language original so that today the two versions can rub shoulders in the country. But still the novel and its characters are still more 'free' in exile in the double sense of both language and country than they are at home in their native country and language.

Matigari is one of my most personal narratives in the sense that in writing it I was trying to experiment with oral narrative forms. I hope readers of the American edition will enjoy the story. They do not have to look beyond their shoulders in the fear that a state authority will haul them in prison for reading a story about a man whose main interest is in the quest for truth and justice.

Ngũgĩ wa Thiong'o
Orange, New Jersey
December, 1997

TO THE READER/LISTENER

This story is imaginary.
The actions are imaginary.
The characters are imaginary.
The country is imaginary- it has no name even.
Reader/listener: may the story take place in the country of
    your choice!

The story has no fixed time.
Yesterday, the day before yesterday, last week . . .
Last year . . .
Or ten years ago?
Reader/listener: may the action take place in the time of
    your choice! .

And it has no fixed space.
Here or there . . .
This or that village . . .
This or that region.
Reader/listener: may you place the action in the space of
    your choice!

And again, it does not demarcate time in terms of seconds
Or minutes
Or hours
Or days.
Reader/listener: may you allocate the duration of any of the
    actions according to your choice!

So say yes, and I'll tell you a story!
Once upon a time, in a country with no name . . .

❖

PART ONE

Ngarũro wa Kĩrĩro

❖

Wiping Your Tears Away

1

He held an AK47 in his right hand. His left hand was raised to shield his face while he looked across the river, as he had often done over many years, across many hills and valleys, in the four corners of the globe. It was all over now, but he knew he still had to be careful.

A riderless horse galloped past him. It stopped, looked back at him for a while and then disappeared into the woods. It reminded him of the horses that Settler Williams and his friends had often ridden as they went to hunt foxes accompanied by packs of well-fed dogs. It felt like so long ago; and yet. . .

How the settlers had loved shedding blood!. . . They would dress in red, and the rider who got to the fox first would cut off its tail in triumph; then he would smear the blood of the fox on the face of a woman. . . Yes, it felt like a long time back. . . Well, there was no night so long that it did not end with dawn. . . He hoped that the last of the colonial problems had disappeared with the descent of Settler Williams into hell.

The sun was just rising, but the land was cloaked in fog. He could not see far and wide around him. He was middle-aged, tall and well-built. He wore a wide-brimmed hat, strapped under his chin, its top decorated with a thin band covered in beads of many colors. His leopard coat, which had now lost most of its original fur, fell on corduroy trousers to his knees. The boots he wore were covered with patches.

He walked along the banks of the river. Then suddenly he saw what he was looking for: a huge *mūgumo,* a fig tree, right in the middle of a cluster of other trees. It was remarkable for its very wide trunk and its four roots were visible, with one jutting out from the middle, and three others sticking out at the sides. He smiled to himself as he stood his AK47 against the tree and drew his sword from where it was hidden beneath his coat. He began digging the ground next to the central root. He covered the bottom of the hole with dry leaves. He now took the AK47, wrapped it in a plastic sheet and carefully laid it in the hole. He washed the sword in the river, put it back in its sheath and then placed it in the hole beside the rifle.

Round his waist he wore a cartridge belt decorated with red, blue and green beads from which hung a pistol in a holster. He slowly unfastened the belt, counted the bullets, rolled it up carefully and then placed it next to the sword and the AK47 rifle. He looked at these things for a while, perhaps bidding them good-bye. He covered them with dry soil. He rubbed off all traces of his footsteps and then covered the spot with dry leaves so skillfully that nobody would have suspected there was a hole there.

He went down to the river and bent to wash his face and hands. So chilly! It reminded him of the other waters in the past which had been just as cold. He remembered how, then, they had sung throughout the night in the open air.

> If only it were dawn,
> If only it were dawn,
> So that I can share the cold waters with the early bird.

The water had numbed their skin, so that none of them felt the pain as the knife cut into the flesh. Before this moment, they were mere boys, but by the time they unclenched their fists, they were men. Their blood mingled with the soil, and they became patriots, ready for the armed struggle to come.*

He rose, turned and one more time looked at the spot where he had buried his weapons, murmuring to himself, "It's good that I have now laid down my arms." He tore a strip of bark from a tree and girded himself with it, once again murmuring, "Instead, I have now girded myself with a belt of peace. I shall go back to my house and rebuild my home." He crossed the river and came out of the forest.

2

He climbed up and down yet other hills and mountains, crossed many other valleys and rivers, trekked through many fields and plains, moving with determination towards the heart of the coun-

---

*A reference to *mararanja* (Gĩkũyũ): a festival of dance and song performed during circumcision. The description also alludes to the initiation ceremony preceding armed struggle.

try. The sun shone brightly. He took off his coat, carried it over his right shoulder and strode on, the sun shining directly into his face. But he still did not waver or look back. Black-eyed susans and other weeds clung to his clothes as though welcoming him back to the fields. He was sweating. So much heat! So much dust! What trials one had to endure on this earthly journey! But there was no arrival without the effort of moving feet.

He tried to visualize his home. In his mind's eye he could see the hedges and the rich fields so clearly. Just another climb, the final climb, and then he would be home — his home on top of the hill!

His feet felt heavy. He decided to rest for a while. He laid his coat on the ground and sat on it in the shade, leaning back against the tree. He removed his hat, placed it on his left knee and wiped his brow with his right hand. His hair was a fine mixture of black and grey. His brow had creased with fatigue. He yawned drowsily. How could it be so oppressively hot so early?

He dozed off. His thoughts took flight. How can I return home all alone? How can I cross the threshold of my house all alone? What makes a home? It is the men, women and children — the entire family. I must rise up now and go to all the public places, blowing the horn of patriotic service and the trumpet of patriotic victory, and call up my people — my parents, my wives, my children. We shall all gather, go home together, light the fire together and build our home together. Those who eat alone, die alone. Could I have forgotten so soon the song we used to sing?

> Great love I saw there,
> Among the women and the children.
> We shared even the single bean
> That fell upon the ground.

He started and woke up. He put on his hat and picked up his coat, which he once again carried over his right shoulder.

An irresistible urge to go and just peep at his house gnawed at him, but he fought against it. He had made up his mind. He would first go in search of his people; at least first find out where they lived, what they ate and drank and what they wore. So many traps, oh so many temptations, in the way of the traveler on this earth!

3

He crossed one more field, went through a cluster of young wattle trees and came to a tarmac road. He stopped and looked first to the right, then to the left. Parked on the other side of the road was a black Mercedes-Benz, with its aerial up. A voice drifted to where he stood:

. . . This is the Voice of Truth. . . All gatherings of more than five people have been banned by a decree of His Excellency Ole Excellence. No explanations were offered for the ban. But it is known that the university students were going to demonstrate outside the British and American Embassies in protest against the continued western military and economic aid to the South African apartheid regime. . .

*

His Excellency Ole Excellence said that a friend in need is a friend in deed. He said this as he bade farewell to the British soldiers who last month disarmed a group of soldiers who had attempted a mutiny. His Excellency Ole Excellence heartily thanked the British government for allowing some of the soldiers to remain to assist with training. Addressing the nation, His Excellency Ole Excellence repeated what he had said during the mutiny: it was a great shame for the soldiers of the national army to go on strike for higher pay so soon after Independence. They had never gone on strike against the colonial regime. Why now?

*

. . . This is the Voice of Truth. The Minister for Truth and Justice has said that this is a workers' government. All workers should disassociate themselves from those who are disrupting industrial peace by demanding increases in wages. Such workers were no better than the soldiers who had disrupted the peace with their attempted mutiny. . .

*

Government bans the Opposition Party. . . His Excellency Ole Excellence has said that this is a people's government. . . The people do not want opposition parties, as they only cause disorder in the country.

4

He walked along the road past the Mercedes, but bits and pieces of news still floated after him. ". . . *United States told Russia that. . . Soviet Union told USA. . . China and India. . . Astronauts. . . Cosmonauts. . . and now for motor racing. . .*" Why could not everybody gird themselves with a belt of peace so that all wars and conflicts on earth would end? In the Mercedes were a black man with a bottle of beer and a black woman with a soft drink.

His thoughts soon drifted from the news to the cars which drove past him. Some had only Europeans in them, others Asians, and others Africans. Long, long before, he had been Settler Williams' chauffeur. "How things and times changed!" he thought. Who could ever have believed that one day Africans would be driving their own cars? Now all that remained for them to do was to manufacture their own cars, trains, airplanes and ships. His thoughts strayed back to his family. Where would he start looking for them?

He came to a police station a few yards from the road. Should I ask for my people at this place? No. I shall do all the searching myself. Further along the road, he caught up with two policemen with an alsatian dog, by the gate of a small council clinic. He walked past them towards the hill under which ran the railway tunnel. His thoughts now turned to the railway and the tunnel. He shivered. How many lives had been claimed by the railway and the tunnel at the time they were built? He remembered the explosions of dynamite and the screams of the workers whenever the walls caved in, often burying them alive. And the groans as some were flattened by the heavy rollers came back to him so vividly that for a time, he thought he could still hear the blood-curdling cries of the dying. After the railway was completed, it had started swallowing up the tea leaves, the coffee, the cotton, the sisal, the wheat — in fact all the produce from all the land that Settler Williams and his like had stolen from the people.

The man stood on top of the hill and looked down. The town spread across the plain below. Hills engulfed the plain on all sides, forming a kind of protective wall around it. His glance moved beyond the hills to the distant horizon, and then back to the town below. How it had grown!

The two policemen with the dog now caught up with him. He watched them go down on the bend of the road towards the town. He now heard the distant siren at the factory, calling out the workers for the ten o'clock break. I wonder if the break is still the five minutes it used to be — just enough time to go to the toilet and relieve yourself quickly or for a few puffs of a cigarette? He thought of all the sirens in all the years gone by. He thought of all those who had lost their limbs, of all those whose bodies and minds and hearts had been battered and broken over the centuries while laboring with their hands. And today? What of today? Some of the words and phrases he had heard on the radio came back. "... *People's government...*" The image of the black Mercedes flashed across his mind; then that of the two policemen and the dog... the clinic... Had anything really changed between then and now? I cannot get to know the answer until I get home. And I will not go home until I have found my people. Where shall I start to look for them? The factory siren wailed again, and his mind became clear as if relieved of a heavy weight. Why hadn't I thought of it before?

The people working in the factory came from all parts of the country. A factory was really the workers' meeting place. Any patriot looking for his people ought to start where people worked.

He walked towards the factory, guided by the smoke issuing from its chimneys. He walked past the post office, the railway station and the rail goods shed.

The black Mercedes he had seen earlier drove past him.

Once again, he caught up with the two policemen. They were now standing at the side of the road near the gate of the factory. Then they moved behind a cluster of wild bushes.

He walked towards the gate.

5

A bill-board with red bold lettering hung on the pillars above the iron gates:

**ANGLO-AMERICAN
LEATHER AND PLASTIC WORKS
PRIVATE PROPERTY
NO WAY**

A wire fence ran around the vast compound. The factory building itself was inside a wall of metal sheeting, while barbed wire fenced the workers' quarters.

A red tractor was coming from the factory. It carted three trailer-loads of rubbish. The guard emerged from behind a post and lifted the barrier to let it through. It headed towards a signpost further up the road: "GREEN MARKET, 200 yards." He drew nearer the gate.

The guard sat on a stool. He wore a khaki uniform and a red fez with a black tassel. On the jacket were the words "Guard, Company Property." At his feet was a tin with charcoal. Why on earth has he lit a fire in this heat? Ill perhaps? Then he saw that the man was only roasting sweet potatoes. The guard, he felt, would be the right person to ask how to go about finding his family in the factory. With so many people in this place, there was bound to be somebody; or perhaps the watchman himself might actually know the children. . . his people.

His thoughts were interrupted by the sound of children's screams and shouts. He turned and saw a whole battalion of children running about in the middle of the road. Why are they running like this? He saw the red tractor making its way back from the market. The trailers were now heaped with more rubbish from the market. But why are the children running away from the tractor? My children. . .!

He did not even talk to the guard. He quickened his pace and followed the children and the tractor. His heart beat wildly. Let me hurry and tell them that I'm back. Let me tell them that the years of roaming and wandering are over. We shall all go home together. We shall enter the house together. We shall light the fire together. After all, the struggle was for the house, wasn't it? A home. . . a shelter. . . with children playing on the verandah or in the open air. . . Sharing what little we have. . . Joy after all that suffering . . . cold . . . hunger . . . nakedness . . . sleepless nights. . . fatigue. . . And how often did we come close to death? Victory is born of struggle. There is no night so long that it does not end with dawn.

He could not believe what he saw. Could such things be possible in this day and age in a country like this? Was this happening in broad daylight?

The children raced the tractor to the garbage yard, a huge hole fenced around with barbed wire. Some vultures perched on the barbed wire, while others sat on branches of trees nearby. Hawks hovered dangerously in the sky. A pack of stray dogs walked about, sniffing here and there at the rubbish. Two men stood at the only entrance to the yard, arranging the children into a queue.

I wonder what they are queuing for! The tractor drove into the yard, with the vultures now hovering over it and dogs running alongside, sniffing in anticipation. A terrible stench filled the air.

The driver tipped the rubbish in three heaps. No sooner had he finished than the dogs, the vultures and the children went scrambling for the heaps of rubbish.

He now understood what was going on. Each child had to pay a fee to enter. A ticket to enable them to fight it out with dogs, vultures, rats, all sorts of scavengers and vermin, for pieces of string, patches of cloth, odd bits of leather, shoe soles, rubber bands, threads, rotten tomatoes, sugarcane chaff, banana peels, bones. . . anything!

He stood there, shocked.

My children?

The two men left together with the tractor as it drove away, leaving behind the din of the children and animals as they scrambled for the rubbish from the market and the factory.

"I've found a radio! I've found a radio!" a boy shouted, jumping up and down with joy.

Within minutes, not an inch of rubbish had been left unturned. Each child now carried a small bundle — bits of thread, papers, plastic sheets, pipes and patches of cloth of all descriptions. Some of the children had stuffed their mouths with rotten tomatoes, while others were busy cleaning bones with their teeth, hoping to find a scrap of meat still clinging to them. And then he saw two boys struggling over a bundle of shoelaces, with the others standing around cheering. The bigger boy knocked down the smaller one, sat on top of him and held him by the throat, strangling him. The smaller boy kicked about wildly but all the time clinging to the bundle of shoelaces.

The man grabbed a stick and ran towards the children. The bigger boy saw him approaching, quickly got off his victim and ran away, stopping at a distance. The little one sat up, felt his neck and looked at the man with gratitude. But when he saw that the man held a stick, this boy too took to his heels.

The man just stood outside the garbage yard. Remembering that he wore the belt of peace, he threw away the stick and followed the children.

He found the two policemen with the dog, the tractor driver and the two men who had collected money from the children in conference behind a bush near the road. They held their heads close together, and money jingled between them. So these five were busy dividing among themselves the money they had taken from the children? So a handful of people still profited from the suffering of the majority, the sorrow of the many being the joy of the few?

It was questions like these which had led him into the forests and the mountains. But that was then. What of today?

A vision of his house appeared before him. He had not been there, he had not yet been home. The urge to go and look at his house seized him with the force of thirst and hunger of many days. But he reminded himself that he had not yet found his people. He could not go home alone.

He hurried after the children.

6

The smaller boy was still afraid of the bigger one. He walked slowly, at a distance behind the others. The man soon caught up with him. The boy was unaware of him until he was right next to him. He was startled.

"Don't be afraid. I've thrown the stick away," the man said.

They walked side by side in silence. The boy's clothes had patches all over them, and his toes could be seen peeping out of the holes in his shoes.

"Why are you following us?" he asked the man. "Do you also want to steal from us the things we found? These are our gains, you know!"

"Gains?" the man asked, not understanding what the boy meant.

"Yes. . . these are our gains, the things we found in the pit," he said, showing him the little bundle of shoelaces.

"Do people steal them from you, then?"

"But of course! When they see that we've found things like shoes, belts, pieces of leather or cloth in good condition, they pretend to get angry, and they growl at us: Where did you get these things from, you little thieves?"

"Who are these people?"

"Adults, people like you or others," the boy replied. Then he giggled a bit and added, "Not so much now, though."

"Why?"

"Oh, we have learned how to deal with them. We pelt them with stones, or wait until we get one of them on their own, and beat them up."

"Why do you pay to enter the garbage yard? Is it a council tax?"

"Of course not. The two men you saw have taken it upon themselves to tax us."

"What happens if you don't pay?"

"Oh, they beat us up."

"Why don't you all beat these two up, or pelt them with stones, or even take them to the police station?"

"The police station? Are you joking? What police? The police and these bandits work together. They are as inseparable as these fingers on my hand," the boy said, holding his hand out to the man. "If we don't pay, the police come after us claiming that we are thieves, or they forbid us from going into the pit under the pretext that we will catch cholera and pass it on to other people. Sometimes they drive us away from our houses and call us vagrants."

"Where do you live?"

"In our houses."

"Your houses? Where?"

"Do you want to see them?"

"Yes."

"Come with me, then."

They walked past the market-place to their left, and on through the shopping center of storied buildings to their right. They walked past the Barclays Bank, American Life Insurance and British-American Tobacco. They went across an open yard next to an Esso filling-station.

"How come there are so many cars parked in this yard?" the man asked the boy.

"These? They are nothing to speak of. If you came here sometimes, you would be surprised. This car-park sometimes fills up with Mercedes-Benzes; you would think that this is where they are manufactured. Their owners drink at the New Sheraton Hotel."

Indeed, much further on one could see a huge four-storied building surrounded by pine trees and by flowers of all colors of the rainbow in full bloom.

"This wasn't here when I was last here," the man said.

"What do you really want?" the boy asked him again. By now the other children had disappeared.

"I am looking for my children."

"Your children? Have they run away from home?"

"No, it was the other way round. I first lost my home; then my children were scattered all over the country."

"When was this?"

"Oh, a long, long time ago."

"Where have you been all this time? Why didn't you look for them before?"

His heart skipped a beat. How was he going to tell this boy that he had spent all his life struggling for a shelter; that he had spent many years fighting Settler Williams for the sake of his children?

He thought of telling the boy the story of his life's struggle with Settler Williams, in the forests, mountains, valleys, ditches, caves, plains, rivers, hills, all over the country.

"I started looking for them long ago," he told the boy.

"But would you recognize them?"

"They look like you, like all the others. You look as if you all came from the same womb. . . same mother, same father."

"I have no father," the boy said. "I hear he was killed fighting for independence."

"Death of a patriot . . ." the man said, like one in a trance. "Martyred for our land, our industries, our homes."

"Where are they?" the boy asked, with no hint of irony or sarcasm in his voice.

"Yes, where are they?" the man echoed, as though he too wanted to know the answer to that question.

The boy interrupted his thoughts.

"You can stop now. Those are our houses."

They were now standing in an open space. They had left the storied buildings behind them. In front of them was a scrapyard where cars of all makes were heaped — Ford, Mercedes, Volkswagen, Peugeot, Volvo, Fiat, Datsun. A scrap-yard, no, a graveyard for motor vehicles: some dented, others so completely wrecked that only their frames remained to tell the tale that here was once a car. Yes, a true vehicle cemetery!

The very badly damaged ones were stuffed with pieces of cardboard, plastic, papers, sacking, cloth, almost anything. Some stood on stones. Others had grass growing inside them.

"That is our village!" he said again.

"These wrecks?"

"Yes, they are our houses. Each one of us has his own house. Mine is a Mercedes-Benz," he announced proudly, as if to say that his house was better than all the others.

Then and now. . . the past and the present. . . yesterday and today. . . what curse befell us? The present and the past. . . his heart beat in rhythm with his thoughts. He wanted to embrace all the children and take them to his house that very moment. Yes, he wanted to take them to that house over which he and Settler Williams had fought for many years, chasing each other through all the mountains and forests of the country. What was that song we used to sing?. . . We would share even the bean which fell on to the ground, the bean that we toiled for. . .? He saw a vision of himself and his children entering their house together, lighting the fire together and working together for their home, smoke drifting from the roof of their common home. The children would come out of this graveyard into which their lives had been condemned. They would build their lives anew in the unity of their common sweat. A new house. A paradise on this earth. Why not? There is nothing that a people united cannot do. Still carried away by his vision, he began walking towards the wrecks, to bear the glad tidings to the children. A new heaven on a new earth.

At the factory, the siren wailed announcing the lunch break. "Don't!" the boy warned. "Visitors are not allowed beyond that point."

Perhaps he did not hear the boy's warning. He continued towards the children's village.

A stone just missed his left eye. The second stone landed at his feet. It was not until the third stone whizzed dangerously close to his face that he realized that they were aimed at him. The bully boy stood on the frame of a Mercedes, telling the others that the man was out to rob them of the things they had found among the garbage.

He stopped in his tracks.

The stones now came flying from all directions. He groped around his waist where he usually had his pistol, but then he remembered he was girded with the belt of peace. He also realized that these were mere children, his children and not the enemy. He stood on the spot stupefied. My children!

The little boy was the first to react. He rushed to him and took him by the hand, pulling him away.

The man followed the boy.

When the children saw him leaving, they jeered and threw more stones with renewed vigor, edging him towards the factory gate. His head and shoulders drooped in sadness. His face creased with age. But he seemed to be protected by a powerful charm, because not a single stone touched him.

Cars carrying European, Asian and African occupants drove by. Some stopped by the roadside to give the passengers a chance to enjoy the scene of children pelting an old man with stones. Some of them stayed inside the cars and watched the drama through the windows. Others sat on the boots or leaned against their cars, sipping their Cokes or puffing their cigarettes. They were not the only observers. Shopkeepers and their customers crowded the doorways or stood in little groups outside.

"Why are they beating that lunatic?" some asked. Others shook their heads and said, "Children and madmen hate each other like Satan and the Cross."

The man did not alter his pace; nor did he seem perturbed in any way by the danger he was in. He shifted his coat from one shoulder to the other.

The factory gateway filled up with the stream of workers filing out for their lunch break. The boy ran in that direction.

The man was now all alone at the center of the three groups: the children, the spectators and the workers.

It was very hot.

Many questions flashed through his mind, but no answer seemed to offer itself. They all culminated in one big question: What curse has befallen us that we should now be fighting one another? That children and their parents should be fighting while our enemies watch with glee?

The magic charm that had earlier protected him seemed suddenly to leave him. A stone caught him on the right ear. He felt his earlobe. His fingers were covered in blood. Another stone knocked off his hat, which fell behind him. He turned around and bent to pick it up. But as he made to straighten up, yet another stone landed on the bridge of his nose. His hat and coat fell off.

He felt his bladder and bowels nearly give way as the excruciating pain shot through his body. Blood flowed from his nose, his mouth and his ears. Like hounds which had smelt blood, the children now pelted him harder with a hail of stones. His head reeled. He sank to the ground and lost consciousness.

The workers streamed past him. All at once the children stopped throwing stones and returned to their village. The car owners too continued on their way. The shopkeepers went about their business, and the workers walked by, talking about the factory, and particularly about the strike they were going to stage that day. They were not interested in an old man lying on the grass.

The boy, who had by now disappeared among the workers, held one of them by the hand and showed him the injured man.

"Why is he bleeding like that?" the worker asked, taking a handkerchief out of his pocket and dabbing at the man's face and ears to remove the blood.

The man opened his eyes. He met the eyes of the boy, filled with pity.

"My child, you didn't forsake me?" he asked.

"No," the boy replied, his eyes cast down at the spot where the man's blood had dripped.

"You will be remembered," the man said. Then he noticed the worker who bent over him, wiping blood off his face.

7

"And who are you, my son?" he asked the man.

"Who, me?" the worker said. "My name is Ngarũro wa Kĩrĩro."

"Ngarũro? Of the Kĩrĩro clan? Thank you. A day will come when we will get to know each other better and stop throwing stones at one another. Would you kindly show us a place where we can shelter from this scorching sun? A place where we could perhaps have a bite, that is, me and . . ."

"Mũriũki. My name is Mũriũki."

"Yes, that's right, a place where Mũriũki and I can find something to eat. Or do you prefer to return to your village?"

Mũriũki hesitated. He could see that the man was really in pain but was trying hard not to betray it.

"I don't know," the boy answered. "If I go back there, the big boy will surely beat me up and steal my things. He is such a big bully. But even the others will punish me for showing you, a stranger, the way to our village, and for allowing you to go beyond the boundary line. I'll have to keep hidden for two or three days until they forget what took place today."

"Do you live in the children's village?" Ngarũro asked.

"Yes, that's where I live," the boy replied.

"Don't worry," the man said, and he sprang abruptly to his feet as though he had recovered such youthful strength as to overcome all the pain. He picked up his things, his eyes shining brightly as if he could see far into the future.

" I will take you to the house. We will go home together so that you can see that it was not for nothing that I spent all these years struggling against Settler Williams . . ."

Ngarūro and Mūriūki looked at each other, wordlessly asking the same question. What had happened to the man's wrinkles?

"What is your name?" Ngarūro wa Kīrīro asked him.

"Matigari ma Njirūūngi."

"Matigari ma Njirūūngi?"

"Yes, that is my name."

They walked towards the market-place in silence.

"Matigari ma Njirūūngi," Ngarūro repeated. "The patriots who survived the bullets?"*

"Ah, you know them, then?"

"I have heard of them."

"What are patriots?" Mūriūki asked.

"Patriots are those who went to the forest to fight for freedom," Ngarūro answered. "People say that some of them remained in the forest."

"What on earth for?"

"To keep the fire of freedom burning," Ngarūro replied.

"But why?"

"So that it does not die out. You know that the fire of freedom was first lit in the forests and mountains," Ngarūro explained.

"That is true," Matigari said. "These children are too young to know. Take me, for example. Settler Williams and I spent many years in those mountains you see over there, hunting one another down through groves, caves, rivers, ditches, plains, everywhere. I would sometimes catch sight of him in the distance, but by the time I was ready to fire, he had disappeared in the bush, and he would be swallowed by the darkness of the forest.

"At other times he would push me into a corner, but by the time he fired, I had already ducked. I would roll on the ground, crawl on my knees or crawl on my belly, and I would thus slip through his fingers. And so, day after day, week after week, month after month, many years rolled past.

Matigari ma Njirūūngi (Gīkūyū): Literally, "the patriots who survived the bullets" — the patriots who survived the liberation war, and their political offspring.

"Neither of us was prepared to surrender. Sometimes I would hit him and think that I had provided him with a ticket to hell. But just as I was about to come out singing songs of victory, news would reach me that he had been spotted elsewhere, searching to destroy me. On other occasions his bullets would catch me. I would crawl, limp and hide in caves to recuperate, waiting for my broken bones to mend. Many were the times he narrowly missed me! It's just that God was not ready to receive me in His kingdom just then. And what do you think we were struggling for?

"A house. My house.

"You see, I built the house with my own hands. But Settler Williams slept in it and I would sleep outside on the verandah. I tended the estates that spread around the house for miles. But it was Settler Williams who took home the harvest. I was left to pick anything he might have left behind. I worked all the machines and in all the industries, but it was Settler Williams who would take the profits to the bank and I would end up with the cent that he flung my way. I am sure that you already know all this. I produced everything on that farm with my own labor. But all the gains went to Settler Williams. What a world! A world in which the tailor wears rags, the tiller eats wild berries, the builder begs for shelter. One morning I woke up from the deep sleep of many years, and I said to him: Settler Williams, you who eat what another has sown, hear now the sound of the trumpet and the sound of the horn of justice. The tailor demands his clothes, the tiller his land, the worker the produce of his sweat. The builder wants his house back. Get out of my house. You have hands of your own, you cruel and greedy one. Go build your own! Who deceived you into thinking that the builder has no eyes, no head and no tongue?

"By now I was trembling like a leaf in the wind. Not because it was cold; not because I was afraid. I was trembling with rage, rage of a newly found dignity that comes from having the scales of a thousand years fall from one's eyes. I was now human.

"Settler Williams leaped to the telephone. I crept slowly to the safe where he kept his gun. I took it, yes, took his gun and releasing the catch, I went on one knee and pointed the gun at him. He was still on the telephone and there I was pointing his gun at him. Wonders will never cease! You wouldn't believe, would you, that it was John Boy, a black man, the settler's servant, who saved him? I have no idea where he suddenly emerged from. Perhaps he came from the kitchen. He jumped on my back screaming. The gun fell to the ground, and he and I started wrestling. I was determined to get the gun. Settler Williams was coming to join John Boy against me, and without the gun I would be no match against the two of them. I drew up all my strength, broke free of John Boy's hold and jumped out through the window. I ran into the tea plantation, through the maize fields, through banana plantations. I crossed rivers, climbed hills and disappeared into the mountains. Settler Williams followed me to see who would silence whom in order to clear any doubts as to who the real master was.

"Thus we spent many years!

"It was only yesterday that the doubts were cleared. Settler Williams fell. I slowly crept up to where he lay, just in case he was pretending to be dead. He was dead. I placed my left foot on his chest and raised his weapons high in the air, proclaiming victory!

"And so today is my homecoming, and I want to bring my family together."

The man's eyes shone brightly. His melodious voice and his story had been so captivating that Mūriūki and Ngarūro wa Kiriro did not realize that they had reached the restaurant. His story had transported them to other times long ago when the clashing of the warriors' bows and spears shook trees and mountains to their roots.

"How many stayed behind to keep the fire of freedom going?" Ngarūro wa Kīrīro asked.

"Ask me another."

"No, I understand. Here we are. This is the restaurant."

The bar was a stone building with a corrugated iron roof. The restaurant was a small extension at the side, built of wood with a canvas roof. Enclosing the whole compound was a wall of cardboard and sacking.

People had their food in the bar and in the restaurant. More sat in the compound. The bill of fare hung on the wall:

MATAHA HOTEL
BAR AND RESTAURANT
Ugali with Roast Meat and Stew; Greens with Maize and Beans; Mashed Peas and Potatoes; Chick-peas; Soya Beans; Tea; Milk; and Porridge; Chapati, Bread, Samosas, Scones, etc.
HERE WE SELL EVERYTHING
EXCEPT WHAT YOU DON'T LIKE.

The workers were now beginning to return to the factory in groups of three, four and five.

"I shan't come in," Ngarũro said. "The workers have decided that we must return early and meet outside the factory. There is to be a strike."

"A strike?" Matigari asked.

"Yes, it starts at two o'clock . . . You will find all the food you want here. Look for some water and wipe the blood off your face. . . I'd better rush. The sun never stops, even for a king!"

"Have you come across or heard of my family at the factory?"

"Matigari's family?" Ngarũro asked. "And whose family do you think we all are?" he said with a faint smile.

"Spread the message: Settler Williams is dead. John Boy is dead. We must go home, light the fire and rebuild our home together."

"Just a moment," Ngarũro said, as a new thought struck him. "Williams? Boy? One of the company directors is called Williams. Robert Williams. His deputy is called John Boy."

"A name can have more than one claimant," Matigari said.

"That is true," Ngarũro answered. "I will give the others your message. This is what I will tell them at the meeting: Williams is dead. John Boy is dead. I will call together all the members of the family and tell them: Let's go home and light the fire together. Let us rebuild our home. The wise among them will understand the hint."

Ngarũro wa Kĩrĩro sprung up as if new strength and confidence had been instilled in him by his brief contact with Matigari.

Matigari and Mũriũki watched him as he strode away and caught up with the train of the other workers. After a while they could no longer single him out from among the others.

The lunch break was nearly over. People could be seen rushing back to work before two o'clock. The two policemen and their dog passed by the restaurant, heading towards the far side of the shopping center.

It was very hot.

Matigari and Mũriũki entered the restaurant, crossed a small gutter and went into the bar.

The wail of the siren filled the air again. It was two o'clock.

8

On the wall were murals of wild animals. An elephant, a hyena, a buffalo, a snake, a leopard and a zebra sat in a circle, all holding a bottle of beer in one hand. King lion sat in the center of the circle, collecting money. On the crown he wore were the words "King of the Jungle." On his belly was the word "Tribute," and at his feet was a barrel with the words "Drink it, Drink It. After All, It Costs So Little, Drink It!"

A fat woman sat behind the counter, protected by a grille. Perched on high stools opposite her were other equally fat women, all dressed in white overalls, talking about the impending workers' strike. "What would we do if the factory closed down?" Their voices were partly drowned by the juke-box blaring out a song: "Shauri Yako".*

Matigari and Mūriūki sat at a table in a corner at the rear of the room. Matigari placed his hat and coat on a seat.

One of the women came from the counter to take their order.

"So now women work in bars?" he asked Mūriūki.

"Women work everywhere now," Mūriūki replied. "They sweep the factories, cut grass in the fields, pick tea, coffee and pyrethrum and clean all the slime from the smelly drains and gutters."

"And your mother? What does she do?"

"I have no mother."

"You have no mother, no father — an orphan? What happened to your mother?"

"She was burned to death when the house was set on fire."

"Set on fire? By whom?"

"The landlord. She used to rent a hut in the village but she could not afford to pay for it. The landlord told her to leave, but my mother asked him: Where will I go if I leave this hut? You can't throw me out into the wilderness like a wild animal. Money isn't more important than life! But the landlord answered: You have to go whether you like it or not. I will see to it myself that you leave. That night, my mother returned home drunk. She went to bed. It was about midnight when I was woken up by the smell of smoke. I ran to where she lay. She was fast asleep. I tried to wake her up. I jumped out through the window, but my mother got stuck because the window was too small. Then the house burst into flames."

---

*Shauri Yako (Kiswahili): "that's your problem".

Matigari brushed off with his hand a fly that buzzed around his ear. The fly did a few more turns in the air before landing next to others on the wall close to the window. He turned and looked at Mũriũki. Will the day come when our orphans can wipe away their tears? he wondered.

One of the barmaids brought them the food and the drinks they had ordered. Mũriũki immediately started sipping his soft drink.

"Don't open the beer yet," Matigari told the waitress. He stood up and went to wash his face at a tap near the toilet. The dried blood on his face made the water that trickled to the ground a little red. He then drank from the tap, filling up his belly with water.

The barmaid went back to where the others sat, and they continued talking about the strike, their half-empty bottles and glasses of beer in front of them. One of the barmaids was crocheting with effortless ease.

The woman who was crocheting suddenly said to the others, "Let us listen to the housewives' program." She walked across the room and turned off the juke-box.

Matigari returned to where Mũriũki sat, busy over his food. Sitting down, he just looked at his own portion without eating it. Many questions crossed his mind. He thought about Mũriũki and about all his people. When he had come out of the forest, he had thought that the task of bringing his family together was going to be an easy one. But now? It was already afternoon, and he had not yet made contact with his own; he did not even know where or how he would begin his search.

The radio came on.

. . .*This is the Voice of Truth. Next on the air is the housewives' program. We shall be talking about family matters today. . . The annual general meeting of the Women's Development Association was opened by the wife of the Minister for Truth and Justice yesterday. Madam the minister's wife, addressing the women, told them that adultery and drunkenness were the principal evils behind the destruction of many homes in the country. Madam the minister's wife urged all women to take refuge in the safety of the church and to stop competing with their husbands in drinking and adultery. Women were the corner-stones of the home, she said.*

Matigari started. Indeed, women were the corner-stones of the

home. How foolish of me not to have thought of it! I should have
started looking for the women. The women would then tell me about
the children. Women are the ones who uphold the flame of conti-
nuity and change in the homestead.

Just as he wondered what to do, he saw a young woman come
into the bar and join the others. They shook hands and clapped one
another's palms jubilantly.

"Hi, Gũthera," they all greeted her together. "What's new?"

"Nothing," she answered, smiling. "I'm just hiding from the cops."

The women behind the counter turned down the volume of the
radio, eager to hear properly what Gũthera had to say.

9

"Why? Have you stolen something?"

"No. It's just that one of the cops is after me. He keeps on following me like I am a bitch on heat. He ought to be ashamed of himself, whistling at me like that in order to make me stop. Who is going
to stop to let cops chat her up, and in broad daylight? Definitely not
Gũthera!"

What a beautiful woman, thought Matigari; a woman with teeth
that gleam white like milk, a mass of hair so black and soft, as if it is
always treated with the purest of oils. Yes, a woman who is neither
too short nor too tall; neither too fat nor too thin. So well built that
her clothes fit her as though she were created in them! See how well
she wears her flower-patterned lasso* around her shoulders so that
the flaps fall gently in soft folds over her shoulders and breasts. It
was difficult not to stare at her. What was such a rare beauty doing
in a dingy bar?

The women burst out laughing.

"What is wrong with the policeman? Don't you like him? Money
is money, you know."

"To me, cops' money stinks of corpses," she answered, turning
while she spoke and noticing Matigari and Mũriũki for the first time.
"I'd rather beg for a beer even from a total stranger — like that man
over there."

Gũthera walked up to Matigari and without much ado sat on his

---

*lasso (Kiswahili): a wrapper.

lap, put her arms around his neck and looked at him with feigned love in her eyes.

"Why do you look at me like that, dad? You've even forgotten to eat your food and drink your beer. I usually drink lager. Go on! Don't be mean! Aren't you going to offer me anything to drink? Or how much do you want to pay for a little pleasure? Pleasures are very expensive, you know. But at this time of the month, the prices are usually low. We even give favors on credit. You can pay at the end of the month. But that is only if you are employed. Are you? Or are you one of those peasants who wait for a cent from the sale of the milk from your one cow? Or perhaps from the sale of coffee picked from your single acre? Or are you the type who ambush their wives for money as they return home after selling their wares in the market-place? Anyway, we don't mind where you get your money from or how. But luck isn't always on our side. For instance, if the factory workers go on strike, I have no clue as to how we will get our food. We might be lucky with those who sell their little plots of land. Would you sell off your wife's plot, or indeed her house?"

"Can't you see that I am old enough to be your father?" Matigari asked Gũthera when he got his first opportunity to say something. "Sit down here on this chair," he said, pushing her off gently with one hand.

She squeezed herself between Matigari and Mũriũki.

"Where have you been living, old man? Have you been living on the moon or in space perhaps? Or are you just playing hard to get? Let me tell you something. These days it does not matter whether it's your father or your son, whether it's your brother or your sister. The most important thing is money. Even if a boy like this one came to me with money in his pocket, I would give him such delights as he has never dreamt of. Or what do you think, my little hero? The only people I have sworn never to have anything to do with are policemen. Are you a policeman? What is your name?"

Before Matigari could answer, Gũthera glanced out through the window and saw the two policemen with their dog. She leaped to her feet.

"Good God! Those hyenas are headed here. . . I don't want the fools to give me any foolishness. But stay put, old man. I'll be back soon, and then you will have to buy me a drink."

Gũthera disappeared through the doorway.

Matigari held his chin, sadly contemplating what had taken place.

Age crept back on his face; the wrinkles seemed to have increased and deepened. How everything had changed. What was this world coming to?

The women at the counter were now talking about Gũthera. . . So talkative, this Gũthera. . . I don't know what she has against policemen. No money bites. . . If I were Gũthera, I would work on him so much that he would end up pawning his police uniform. . . They continued in this way, just killing time with small talk. They were suddenly startled by the bloodcurdling growl of a dog, followed by the chilling scream of a woman. The barmaids ran out, followed by Mũriũki. The dog continued growling. The woman's screams were of pure terror. Mũriũki returned to the bar, trembling from head to heel.

"It's. . . the. . . woman. . ." he said.

"What's happened?"

"They are setting the dog on her."

"Who are?"

"Those policemen."

Matigari shot out of his seat and darted outside, followed by Mũriũki. What a sight before him!

A crowd of people stood around Gũthera, watching the policemen unleash terror on the woman. She was kneeling on the ground. The dog would leap towards her; but each time its muzzle came close to her eyes, the policeman who held the lead restrained it. Gũthera's wrapper lay on the ground. Each time she stood up to retreat, the dog jumped at her, barking and growling as though it smelled blood. Some people laughed, seeming to find the spectacle highly entertaining.

A gush of urine rushed down her legs; she was staring death in the face.

A feeling of sharp pain and anger flashed through Matigari. His hand moved to his waist in a gesture he had often performed during his years of struggle with Settler Williams in the mountains. There was nothing there. No guns. He remembered that he was now wearing the belt of peace. But he was very angry. Of what use is a man if he cannot protect his children? However, he did not wrap up his anger in silence. It is no use getting angry about things, he had always told himself, if you have no intention of doing something to change them. He turned to the crowd and shouted angrily:

"What is going on here? Are you going to let our children be made to eat shit while you stand around nodding in approval? How can you stand there watching the beauty of our land being trodden down by these beasts? What is so funny about that? Why do you hide behind a cloak of silence and let yourselves be ruled by fear? Remember the saying that too much fear breeds misery in the land."

By now all eyes were on Matigari. The crowd parted as they would to give way to a lunatic. Matigari, without changing his pace, now pointed a finger at the policemen and told them, "Leave her alone!"

"Who gives you the right to interfere with the law?" the police-man who held the dog asked him.

"What kind of law is this which allows policemen to harass defenseless women?"

The policeman became uneasy, since he did not know who this man was or what was making him so confident.

"Do you know that this woman has disobeyed police orders to stop? We are here to ensure peace and stability," the policeman who held the dog said.

"The peace and the stability to ensure theft and robbery? Why don't you admit that it's because she won't open her legs for you that you are harassing her?"

"Do you want me to set this dog loose on you?" the policeman asked menacingly and angrily because he had been exposed. "Do you want me to let this dog tear you up into shreds until you bleed to death?"

"Just you dare try. You will know exactly whom you are dealing with."

"And who are you?" the other policeman asked.

"Matigari ma Njirũũngi."

The courage of truth had once again transformed him. It seemed to have wiped age off his face, making him look extremely youthful.

The first policeman made as if to let the dog loose on Matigari, but the other one took him by the hand and whispered to him:

"Let's go. Have you ever heard of anyone with a name like that? Besides, he might even be an eminent person dressed plainly. Or why do you think he is so bold?"

"*Wewe mwenda wazimu,**" the policeman with the dog told Matigari. "And you, woman, you must learn to obey those whose duty it is to ensure peace and stability."

**Wewe mwenda wazimu:* (Kiswahili): "you are crazy".

The policemen moved away towards the storied buildings at the shopping center.

Matigari walked up to the woman and placed a hand on her shoulder.

"Get up . . . Come, stand up, mother . . ." he said simply.

Gũthera was trembling like a leaf. She stood up slowly, picked up her lasso and walked away uncertainly. Heavy thoughts weighed on her mind.

The rest of the people headed off in all directions, discussing what had taken place. They talked about the policemen, the dog, about Gũthera and Matigari. They asked one another: Who is Matigari?

10

Matigari and Mũriũki went back inside the bar. The women were all busy talking about the incident that had just occurred. Such a thing had not been seen in these parts. One of the barmaids opened Matigari's beer.

"Bring Mũriũki a soft drink," he said to her.

He sat staring at nothing, not eating, not drinking. His thoughts seemed far, far away.

Gũthera came back into the bar. She had washed herself and changed her clothes and lasso. All the barmaids ran towards her and hugged her, telling her how sorry they were about the whole incident. She freed herself from their embraces and walked up to Matigari. She stood next to him humbly. When she spoke, it was with a voice that trembled.

"I don't know who you are . . . but I beg you to forgive me for all the things that I said to you earlier on. I will never forget what you have just done for me as long as I live."

"Take a seat," Matigari said to her. "Ask for something cool to drink, for it is rather too hot."

Gũthera sat facing Matigari and Mũriũki. She ordered a beer. Mũriũki asked for another drink. The barmaid also brought another beer for Matigari.

"I only asked for one beer," he said. "But just leave it here. I'm sure we will find someone to drink it."

They sat sipping their drinks in silence. Even the barmaids lowered their voices.

"What's all this between you and the police?" he asked her.

She hesitated, eyeing Mũriũki, wondering whether or not to speak in his presence. She decided to go ahead.

"I have never spoken about this to anyone," she began. "But ask yourself, what am I doing in the bar? First let me tell you a story . . .

"Long ago, there was a virgin. Her mother had died at childbirth. This girl and her sisters and brothers were brought up by their father. He was a Christian — in fact, a church elder. The girl grew up in the church, as it were. She belonged to the Church of Scotland, whereas her father belonged to the Independent Church. But her father was not opposed to her belonging to this church. He said that what mattered was God's word and His commandments, and not the differences that any two churches may have had. The real Church of God resided in people's hearts. The rest were mere edifices. The girl in question loved two people dearly: her heavenly Father who had given her life, and her earthly father who had brought her up with so much love. Her earthly father really loved children.

He would never eat his supper before all his children had had enough to eat. He had no preference for one child over another. To him all children were God's children, His creatures, and they were all equal. The girl always went to church and never forgot to say her prayers. There in the church, the Ten Commandments were read and taught to her. When she grew older, she was able to read them for herself. She was told to keep them at all times and places.

Thou shalt have no other gods before me.
Thou shalt not make unto thee any graven image:
Thou shalt not take the name of the Lord thy God in vain.
Remember the sabbath day, to keep it holy . . .
Honour thy father and thy mother . . .
Thou shalt not kill.
Thou shalt not commit adultery. Thou shalt not steal.
Thou shalt not bear false witness against thy neighbor.
Thou shalt not covet thy neighbor's things . . .

"Her aim and purpose in life were to do no ill. She aspired only to do good to others. She wanted to tread the paths of virtue and righteousness only.

"She became a born-again Christian. She started praising the Lord so earnestly she felt as though she had grown wings of holiness and could just fly to heaven. Then the war broke out. People became divided. Some of them were patriots, and the others were sell-outs. The world seemed upside-down. Children turned against their parents, parents against their children. Sister and brother swore to take each other's lives. But this girl paid heed to two masters only: her heavenly Father and her earthly one. She was ready to do all she could to serve them. Her father went to church regularly, but he was also a patriot. The girl never knew this, although her father often said to her: Those Ten Commandments are all good, but they are all contained in this one commandment: Love. And there is no greater love than this: that a man should give up his life for somebody else. Imagine, a people ready to give up their lives for one another, for their country. One day, her earthly father was arrested. She went to see him in prison. She went to the superintendent of police to ask why her father had been arrested. He told her: Your father was found carrying bullets in his Bible. The girl denied this. Go ask your father, they said. They brought him in, handcuffed. When she saw him like this, she began to cry. The police officer left her for a while. Is it true? she asked him. Yes, for there is no greater love than this: that men and women should give up their lives for the people by taking to the mountains and forests. This is the greatest commandment of all Christ's commandments, and of all the religions on earth from that of Muhammad to that of Buddha. The girl was greatly shocked and for a while remained speechless. Being found in possession of bullets carried with it a death sentence. They took her father back to his cell. The superintendent came out, smiling slyly. He said: "My superiors do not know about this yet. We can settle this matter between us here and now. Give me your purity, and I will give your parent back to you." The young maiden remained silent. The superintendent explained further. "You are carrying your father's life between your legs.

"The girl went back home and knelt in prayer to the heavenly Father, pleading with Him for guidance. Next morning, she paid the priest a visit. He opened the Bible and read the Ten Commandments to her. Thou shalt have no other gods before me. Thou shalt not kill. Thou shalt not commit adultery. And so on. Honour thy father and thy mother. That is where the real test lay. Thou shalt not commit adultery; honor thy father and thy mother. They knelt down together in prayer. The priest asked the heavenly Father to give courage to this servant, so that she would always walk in the paths of virtue and of righteousness. The following day, the girl went back to the police station. Again the superintendent told her: Your father is among those who call themselves patriots. He has been assisting the terrorists with supplies of bullets. The crime of being found in possession of bullets without a license carries a death sentence. But I shall help you. Nobody outside this police station knows about this. You can trade your innocence for your father's life." The girl answered, "I will never forsake my Father, Creator of heaven and earth. He lay down the commandment: Thou shalt not commit adultery." The police officer told her — Say good-bye to your father, then. Her earthly father was killed. Their land was confiscated by the colonial government, and the girl was left to fend for her brothers and sisters. Problems began to heap on problems. Poverty, the clothes got tattered, and there was no food. Nothing. The other children cried, Where is our father? What shall we eat? The girl just stared at them blankly. The thought that she might have perhaps saved her father's life tormented her. The anguished cry of the children was tearing her apart. And now am I going to watch my sisters and brothers die of hunger? Will I let the blood of my father's house stain my hands? She turned the thought over and over again in her mind. But her heavenly Father would not answer her questions. All that the Bible said was simply: Thou shalt not steal; thou shalt not covet thy neighbor's things; thou shalt not commit adultery. What of hunger? No answer. What of thirst? Again, no answer. What about nakedness? Silence. And at home, the children were still crying, What shall we eat? When will father come back? Where did he go to?

"The girl went back to the priest. She pleaded with all the other Christians in her church. When they saw her approaching, they fled. A terrorist's child? She would go to church, only to return home empty handed.

"One day, the girl decided to walk the streets. That day, she returned home with a packet of flour. Let me tell you this: From the day that she decided to walk the streets, she was able to feed and clothe the other children. But she could not earn enough to send them to school or to a place where they could learn useful skills. Are they not the ones that I meet in bars and shopping centers eating rubbish from the garbage pits, or begging from tourists on street corners? That is the end of my story. But perhaps I have not answered your questions yet. The night that the girl began walking the streets, she swore to herself: Even though it's my troubles which have led me away from the paths of righteousness, and have turned me into a hunter of men, I will never go to bed with a policeman. I will take money from strangers, thieves, murderers even, but I will never open my legs for any policeman, these traitors, no matter how much they are prepared to pay for the favors. This will be my eleventh commandment."

"There are two types of believers," Matigari said, breaking the silence that followed the end of Gūthera's narrative. "Those who love their country, and those who will sell it. There are also two types of soldiers. Some are there to protect the people, others to attack them."

"I have never seen even one of them protecting the people!" she said.

"And what of your father? Such a patriot. A servant of the people! There are also two types of people in the land: those who sell out, the traitors, and those who serve the people, the patriots."

"What is your name?"

"Matigari ma Njirūūngi."

"A patriot? Are you one of those left behind in the forest to keep the fire of freedom alive? Where do you come from?"

"I returned from the forest only this morning."

"What?"

"Yes, I returned from the mountains at dawn."

"And who is he?" Gūthera asked, turning to Mūriūki.

"I found him by the garbage yard," Matigari said.

"Really?" she asked, again turning to Mūriūki. "Are you one of the children who live in the vehicle cemetery?"

"Yes," he said.

"What are you doing here in the bar?" she now asked Matigari. "Have you no home you could return to?"

"I'm looking for my people so that we may go home together."

"The family of the patriots who survived the war?"

"Maybe they do not know who they are yet. Maybe they forgot who they really were. So I will have to go to all the marketplaces, to all the shopping centers and to all the meeting places, and blow the trumpet to call together the family of all the patriots who survived. I will tell them: Settler Williams is dead; let us go home now."

"Settler Williams? Who is he?"

It was now Matigari's turn to tell Gūthera his story: how he had cleared the bush; how he had cultivated and sowed; and how later he had built a house. And all this time Settler Williams had strolled about with his hands in his pockets, whistling tunes or giving orders here and there. He told her how, when he had finished building the house, Settler Williams had grabbed it. He had done the same with the factories. Matigari was the one who produced everything. But it was Settler Williams who collected the profits. Imagine: the tiller dying of starvation, the builder sleeping on the verandah; the tailor walking about without clothes and the driver having to go for miles on foot. How could such a world be? Matigari told Gũthera of how he had fought Settler Williams and of how John Boy saved the settler's life. He explained how he had run to the forests and up the mountains, with Settler Williams and John Boy in pursuit and how thereafter they had hunted one another across all the mountains and valleys.

"It was only yesterday that he fell, and I stood on his chest with my left foot, holding up the weapons of victory and singing victory in my heart: The house is mine now, it belongs to me and my family. . . That is why I am now looking for my people, my daughters, my sons, my in-laws, my wives. . ."

"Even your wives? Where did you leave them?" Gũthera asked him in a tone suggesting she doubted his sanity. "Why does he talk such nonsense!"

"Where could I have left them, my child? That is why I took up arms and retreated into the forests and mountains to fight, so that they could have a home. But I have a problem. Where do I find them now? Where do I start looking?"

"Have you been to the plantations yet?" Gũthera asked, feeling slightly ashamed of having thought ill of him, especially when she remembered how he had saved her from the police dog.

"So they still slave on the plantations?" Matigari asked.

"What do you expect them to do? Today there is no corner of the land where you'll not find women looking for something with which to quell the hunger of their children and husbands," she said. "Most of the women are casual laborers in the tea, coffee and sisal plantations. If you want to know where to begin your search, go to the plantations. Go and rescue those; don't worry about us, for we lost our souls in these bars a long time ago."

"But there are so many plantations. Which one shall I begin with?" Matigari asked, almost speaking to himself.

Gũthera contemplated the question for a while. Throughout

their conversation she had been wondering how she could express her gratitude for what he had done for her. Now was her chance, and she seized it. Whether he was crazy or not was beside the point. She thought: I will go with him, support him, until he finally finds his people.

"Come, let me guide you to the nearest plantation," she told him. "Besides, it will be much easier for me to seek information from the women."

"Let us go at once," he said, standing up. "Let us go before it gets dark."

He still had not eaten or taken his drink. One of the barmaids wrapped up the food in a piece of paper. Matigari took the package and the unopened bottle of beer and put them inside his coat pockets.

11

Although by now the sun had moved a great deal westwards, and the shadows had lengthened, it was still oppressively hot all over the country. The grass wilted, and the leaves wore a tired look about them. The haze in the air was uncomfortable; one saw mirages on tarmac highways. Except for the noise of cars on the road, and that of birds singing in the trees, the whole land was gripped in a deathly stillness. No wind blew. No leaves rustled. No clothes fluttered anywhere.

Three army trucks and four police Land-Rovers went by. The soldiers were fully armed with rifles and machine-guns. The police carried truncheons, shields and tear-gas masks.

"Where are they going?" Matigari asked.

"To the factory," Gũthera replied. "The workers' strike was due to start at two o'clock."

"Are they going to fight against the workers?" he asked.

This man has indeed spent a long time in the forest, she thought to herself. He should first go home and sleep off the fatigue of many years. Who but a stranger would not know that the police in this country were always fighting against students and workers?

"Of course. That's what the police are always doing," Mũriũki answered. "Wasn't it only the other day that the workers were badly beaten, and some of them had their legs broken?"

"We'd better hurry before the women leave the fields," Gũthera urged.

They stood on a hill near a cluster of wattle trees. Before them spread a tea plantation, extending far into the horizon. The tea-bushes were so well trimmed that they now looked like a huge bed of green.

"So fertile, this land!" Gũthera said.

"Does all this land belong to one person?"

"Yes. . . or to foreign companies."

Because they did not know where on the plantation they would find the workers, they decided to walk down between the rows of the tea-bushes, looking out for them. They walked and walked and walked down the slope, but they were still nowhere near the end of the estate. One ridge simply gave way to the next.

Mũriũki felt tired and ached all over. When he looked at Matigari, he could not help wondering: What sort of man is this? I haven't seen him eat or drink anything, and he does not look in the least tired.

After they had walked for several miles without reaching even one of the ends of the plantation, Gũthera suggested that they first find a place where they could spend the night, and continue with their search the following day.

"Look, it's nearly sunset. . . The women have left their work-places by now. . ."

They turned off the track and now started searching for a way out of the plantation. It was not an easy task. They walked through the tea-bushes without finding their way out or coming across anyone who would tell them which way to go. The whole plantation spread out uniformly and endlessly in all directions. No landmarks, not even a cloud of smoke somewhere, broke the green monotony.

Matigari felt sad. The day was about to end. He had not yet found his wives. He had not set eyes on his house. Age seized him. His pace slackened, and he merely dragged his feet along.

They walked westwards, with the rays of the setting sun shining directly into their faces. The heat of the sun was now less intense, but still there was not even the slightest breeze to cool the sweat that clung to their armpits and moistened their brows. Their feet throbbed, and their toes ached.

"This plantation is so big that the owner can cover it from end to end only on horseback."

"Or maybe on a winged car," Mūriūki added, picturing in his mind their yard. "Oh, how I would love to fly above this tea estate on a winged Mercedes-Benz or, better still, on a winged horse, with the leaves of these bushes softly brushing the dust off my aching feet. . ."

Wonders will never cease! Was this a hallucination caused by the sun shining directly into their faces or brought about by the fatigue they felt? For all of a sudden the three of them saw, or thought they saw — a group of horses galloping westwards, leaving behind them a trail of dust goldened by the rays of the setting sun.

"Look, there, through the cloud of dust! Aren't those horses?" Gūthera asked, fascinated by the strange sight.

They followed in the trail of the horses, although they could not see them clearly. The horses continued galloping westwards. A red cloud enveloped the sun, but the sun continued to peep from behind it, sending out darts of fire in every direction.

It turned out that what had seemed like a group was in fact only two horses. Again, they could not see them very clearly, but they could hear and follow the sound of their hoofs. Suddenly Matigari stopped in his tracks and dramatically pointed to a distant hill in front of them, his whole body trembling with excitement.

"The house. . . there is the house. . .!" he exclaimed, his voice trembling in tune with the rest of his body.

"Where?" Gūthera and Mūriūki asked simultaneously.

"There, on the hill!"

Gūthera and Mūriūki strained their eyes to look; and indeed, there on top of the hill overlooking the whole country stood a huge house which seemed to stretch out for miles, as if, like the plantation itself, it had no beginning and no end.

"Is that house really yours?" Gūthera asked doubtfully.

"Yes. . . that's it. . .! That is the house for which I spent so many years struggling against Settler Williams — until yesterday, when he fell and I placed my foot on his chest. . . How could I not have recognized this plantation, recognized my own? Let us go; let us go home together. . ." Matigari said.

His eyes shone brightly. All the creases on his face had gone, and youth had once again returned to him.

12

A white man and a black man sat on horseback on one side of the narrow tarmac road next to the gate. Their horses were exactly alike. Both had silky brown bodies. The riders too wore clothes of the same color. Indeed, the only difference between the two men was their skin color. Even their postures as they sat in the saddle were exactly the same. The way they held their whips and the reins — no difference. And they spoke in the same manner.

They were about to part.

"See you at the party tonight."

Just as they were about to ride off, they saw Matigari walking towards them. They checked their horses and waited.

Gũthera and Mũriũki had already stopped behind a cluster of bushes, and they watched from a safe distance to see what was going to happen. They were each asking themselves the same question: Is this man sane? Were these not the houses which had once belonged to the colonialist settlers but now belonged to the very rich, the foreign and the local people of all colors — black, brown and white? Yet Matigari seemed to have no qualms or any inhibitions. He walked past the two men on horseback and reached for the gate.

"Hey, *mzee,**"the black man shouted. "Can't you see that sign? *Hakuna njia.†* Ha-ha-ha!. . . Or can't you read? That isn't the way to the servants' quarters."

Matigari turned, looked at him for a while and then asked him, "Is that where the keys are?"

"What keys?"

"The keys to this house. . . this home!"

"Which house? Which home?"

"This house!"

"What do you need the keys for?"

"To let myself into the house. I have wandered for far too many years in far too many places over the earth."

"So you think that this is a hotel?" the black man said with angry sarcasm. *"Bob, come and listen to a bloke who claims that my house belongs to him."‡*

---

* *Mzee* (Kiswahili): "old man".

† *Hakuna njia* (Kiswahili): "no way".

‡ Italics here indicate that English, not Gĩkũyũ, is being spoken.

The black man now got off his horse; with one hand on the reins, he walked towards Matigari. His white companion, still on horseback, came nearer. Matigari held the gate with one hand.

"*Is he all right?*" the white man asked the black man. "*Amuse him a little, eh? A piece of comic theater, eh? I will be the audience and you two the actors.*"

"*I was ever such a poor actor,*" the black man said. "*And I would prefer a tragic role. But to amuse you, I'll try. . .* Who are you?" he now asked Matigari.

"Matigari ma Njirũũngi."

"Matigari ma Njirũũngi?"

"Yes."

"And what do you want?"

"The key to my house."

"Do you know whose house it is? Do you know whose home this is?"

"Of course I do! It's mine. It belongs to me and to all my people."

"*Bob, he says that the house is his and his family's. . .* How is it yours?" He now spoke condescendingly to Matigari, as a sober policeman would question a drunkard.

The question "How is it yours?" triggered other memories in Matigari, and his thoughts transported him back to distant places, years before. He let out a sigh. Letting go of the gate, he turned to the black man and began talking to him. Now it seemed as if it was Matigari who was explaining complex things to a child, in a language which only a child would understand. He was not condescending, however, but tolerant and gentle.

"My child, did you ask me how this house was mine? It is a long story. . . there is so much to tell. . . Do you see this house? Do you see these tea plantations and this road? Who do you think built them all? And, mark you, I did not begin yesterday. I have seen many things over the years. Just consider, I was there at the time of the Portuguese, and at the time of the Arabs, and at the time of the British —"

"Look, I don't want history lessons! I only asked you about the house."

"This house? Do you think that this house has a story different from the story of these hands? Hands are the makers of human history. Do you know Settler Williams? The white colonialist who used to live here?"

"*Bob, the fellow claims to know your dad.*"

"*My father? He disappeared in the forest years ago. Fate unknown, but presumed dead.*"

"*Yes, together with my old man. Don't I know?*"

"*Ask him what happened to them. This play is more interesting than our evening rides.*"

The black man once again turned to Matigari and asked him, "Williams? Howard Williams? The white man who lived here?"

"That's the one."

"Yes, I've heard of him. What about him? What do you know of him?"

"You ask me what do I know of him? The white-man-who-reaps-where-he-never-sowed? How can I, black-man-who-produces, not know the white-man-who-reaps-where-he-never sowed? Or how do you think the whole quarrel began? Yes, it was the very fact that I had come to know who he really was that began it all. Right there. Just like that. You can imagine it. One early morning, I woke up, cleaned my ears and eyes and then went to Settler Williams; and I told him. You clan of parasites, there is no night so long that will not end with dawn. And no day dawns like another. Today is a new day, and the sun is shining brightly in the sky. Let me ask you a few questions. Who built this house? Who cleared and tilled this land? Listen to me carefully. The builder demands back his house, and the tiller his land. Who does the white-man-who-reaps-where-he-never-sowed think he is? Does he think that he is God's representative here on earth? Go home. For, from this day on, the builder refuses to beg for a place where he can lay his head; the tiller refuses to starve; the tailor refuses to go without clothes; and the producer refuses to part with his wealth. I sang:

> You foreign oppressor,
> Pack your bags and leave!
> For the owner of this house
> Is on his way!

"When he heard this song, the settler ran to the telephone, and I rushed to the safe to get the gun. . . But there is nothing worse than slavery in this world. Slavery! Ah, slavery! The chaining of the mind and of the soul! Who do you think it was that screamed to warn Settler Williams? Who do you think it was that leaped on my back, making me drop the gun before I could pull the trigger? None other than John Boy!"

"Boy? John Boy? Do you know him also?" the black man asked, startled.

"Who in this country doesn't know John Boy? He used to be the settler's cook. That man! He was really fat — as fat as a pig; no, like a hippo. But what do you expect from anybody feeding on the left-overs from the settler's table —?"

Crack! Crack!

Matigari felt as though his body had been cleaved into two. His muscles gave way. He sank to the ground. None of those present expected to see such a thing take place. Even Gūthera and Mūriūki were taken unawares by the sound of the whip as it shot through the air and landed with a sharp cracking sound on Matigari.

As the black man raised the whip a third time, the white man intervened.

"*What's the matter?*" he asked, still remaining on horseback.

"*Insulting the memory of my late father. . . to my face! Oh, the cheek. . .*"

"*Does he know him also? Didn't he also disappear at the same time as my dad?*"

"*Yes. And this scarecrow seems to know everything. I'll flay him until he squeals everything.*"

"*Cool it. Remember you are playing a comic role; the tragic role was played by our fathers. Ask him a few more questions. Maybe he will provide the missing link in my theory about the fate of my father.*"

Matigari reached towards his waist. Then he remembered that he had girded himself with the belt of peace. He tried his best to endure the pain without letting it show; getting up slowly from where he lay, he held on to the gate for support.

The sun had set by now, but it had left behind a blood-red glow in the evening sky, lighting up the house, the gate and the road on which they stood.

"You've dared to raise a whip against your own father?" Matigari said, still clinging on the gate.

"You're not my father! Take a proper look at me, before darkness sets in. I am John Boy Junior. Mr. Boy, whom you are insulting, happened to be my father. He was a man of class, an important man. He was very wise, and he had great foresight. He sent me to school, at a time when people here did not know the value of education. He put me on a ship and sent me to Fort Hare in South Africa. Then I went to England, where I studied at the London School of Economics, better known as LSE. There I got a number of diplomas in administration. I used to eat *dinners in the Inns of Court,* where I learned how to dress like a gentleman, and from where I was called to the bar. And just as I was about to return home and show my many degrees and certificates to my father, I received a letter informing me that he had gone to the forest with Major Howard Williams, to hunt down terrorists. That—"

"Stop. . . just stop there!" Matigari said, trembling with new excitement. "Are you the boy we sent abroad? The boy the cost of whose education we all contributed to, singing with pride: Here is one of our own and not a foreigner's child over whom I was once insulted? The boy for whom we sang: He shall come back and clean up our cities, our country, and deliver us from slavery? The boy we sent off to study, saying that a child belongs to all, that a nation's beauty was borne in a child, a future patriot?"

"Listen to me carefully. *Mzee,* I would ask you to learn the meaning of the word 'individual'. Our country has remained in darkness because of the ignorance of our people. They don't know the importance of the word 'individual,' as opposed to the word 'masses'. White people are advanced because they respect that word, and therefore honor the *freedom of the individual,* which means the freedom of everyone to follow his own whims without worrying about the others. Survival of the fittest. But you black people? You walk about fettered to your families, clans, nationalities, people, masses. If the individual decides to move ahead, he is pulled back by the others. What's the meaning of the word 'masses'? *Mzee,* let me tell you that what belongs to the masses is carried in a bottomless pail. How does the song go? 'Go your way and let me go mine, for none of us is carrying the other.' — My father knew this; that's why he sent me to school and ignored the idiots who were mumbling nonsense about sharing the last bean."

"Wonders will never cease! Don't you remember how people contributed money to send you to study? Has nobody ever told you? Don't you remember that you intellectuals are greatly indebted to the very masses whom you are now calling idiots?"

"Where did you sign a contract with my father, so that I can pay your money back at once?" John Boy Junior shouted as if he were now addressing a huge crowd. "Yes, where is the contract? I will pay back your money this instant, plus interest. . .! Let me tell you, old man, what is mine is mine. If you want me to share what you have, that's up to you. Go fetch it. I shan't disappoint you. Get up and go home before you land yourself into serious trouble. The sun has already set, and darkness will soon cover the land. The play is over. You'd better leave now in one piece. This house belongs to another."

"To another, besides the builder? I am that builder."

"This fellow is adamant that the house is his," the black man now said to Robert Williams. *"I'm going to end this monkey business. We shall otherwise be late for the party for those making arrangements for the minister's visit tomorrow."*

"I agree," Robert Williams said. *"And I have to find out the latest about the strike. Tell him to piss off. Or, better still - ha-ha-ha-ha! - why don't you ask to see his title-deed to the house? His house! -a-ha-ha-ha! "*

"Do you have the title-deed to this house?"

"My hands are the surest title-deed there ever was. What other deed do you need that is greater than the blood that I shed?"

"I'll give you some advice. This is my house. This house and the land around it are mine. They were sold to me by the son of Howard Williams, this one you see here."

"Him?"

"Yes. He is the first born of Williams. He is a somebody. Yes, watch out, for he is not just anybody. He is a director of Anglo-American International Conglomerate of Insurance (AICI) and Agribusiness Co-ordinating International Organization (ACIO); and he is also a director of the local branch of Bankers' International Union (BIU)* We are both members of the board of governors of the leather and plastic factory. The Minister for Truth and Justice is coming to pay a visit tomorrow. The estate you see across the road belongs to Robert Williams. Is everything clear, old man? Do you now understand who this is? He is my witness because he

---

*The abbreviations here make words in the Gĩkũyũ language: *Aici:* thieves; *Acio:* those; *Biũ:* thorough; hence, "the real thieves."

sold this house to me."

"Is this really the boy who hardly knew how to blow his nose? Who gave him the right to dispose of our land, our factories, our homes, our inheritance? Where did you two meet? We used to think that you educated ones would stand firmly against the whites-who-reap-where-they-have-not-sown. What did you do in Europe? Where did this friendship between you and the clans of the white parasites come from?"

Robert Williams and John Boy drew their heads together and whispered to each other. Then Williams turned his horse and rode away. Matigari began to open the gate and let himself into the compound. John Boy said:

"Wait a minute, old man! Since you said that you don't have the title-deed, how can we know that this house is really yours?"

He spoke sarcastically, but Matigari ignored that. An irresistible desire to enter the house had suddenly gripped him and this had transported him back to the years of struggle, sweat, fatigue, rain, wind, pain and all the suffering that he had been through.

"Come!" he said, looking straight at John Boy. Matigari had a quality about him, a kind of authority in his voice and demeanor, which made people listen to him. Now he and John Boy faced each other as though weighing up one another to see who was the braver. "Come, let us go to the house, and I will show you all the nooks and crannies of my house, take you round all the rooms of this house for which I've suffered so. Come, my people, one and all, let us enter the house together; for my heart has neither envy nor selfishness!" Matigari now said in a raised voice as if addressing a huge crowd. "Yes, come all, and let us light a fire in the house together! Let us share the food together, and sing joyfully together!"

Just as he was about to open the gate, Matigari heard the sound of an engine. Next he saw headlamps. A Land-Rover stopped where they were. Two policemen jumped down, leaving another in the back, holding the leash of a dog.

"*Wapi ule mwivi**?", one of the two policemen asked.

Robert Williams returned to the spot on horseback. Williams the white man and Boy the black man both pointed at Matigari. The policemen jumped at Matigari and shone a torch in his face.

---

*Wapi ule mwivi (Kiswahili): "where is that thief?"

"*Ni ule mzee! Ni ule mzee*!*" one of them said.

They were the same policemen Matigari had encountered earlier that afternoon.

"Are you crazy or what?" asked the one who had earlier harassed Gũthera.

They lifted him bodily and flung him into the Land-Rover like a log. The dog growled ferociously and gnashed its teeth.

"See you at the party," John Boy and Robert Williams said as they parted.

The policemen drove away. Gũthera and Mũriũki emerged from their hide-out behind the bush.

13

Matigari was flung into a small dark cell which reeked with the breath of the ten other people packed there. The heavy odor of vomited beer, the smell of the sweat on their bodies and that of the human sweat and blood which had dried up on the walls of the cell over the years made it hard for him to breathe. He fought back with difficulty the nausea that seized him. The cell was silent but for the regular sound of a drunkard snoring as he lay in his own vomit.

One of the inmates began to shout, "Help! Who's pissing?"

"It's the drunkard!" a number of voices answered together.

The prisoners pushed into one another, trying to escape the jet of urine, but there was no space left into which they could move. Some made noises of disgust, and others shouted,

"First he retches! Then he pisses!"

"Now all that's left for him to do is shit on us!"

"Pinch him!"

"Punch him!"

"Wake up, *wewe punda milia!*"† One of them punched him. He woke up.

"Why are you showering us with your urine?"

"And farting like an old hog?"

"Who me?" the drunkard asked, still bemused with sleep and alcohol. "I was just helping God."

---

*Ni ule mzee (Kiswahili): "it's that old man."

†*Wewe punda milia* (Kiswahili): "you zebra."

"To fart and vomit and urinate?" another said.

"I swear I was just helping God to make it rain. Can't you see how the drought has spread across the country? Just feel these walls or the floor, how parched they are. You see, as I stood by the road, all I could see on either side was dry grass, dry weeds and dry trees. Then I asked myself: How come the whole country is so dry? I then thought: if I let one or three drops fall, the Almighty might have mercy and follow my example and let a bit of His pee fall to benefit us all in the country."

"So your vomit was some kind of sacrifice to God?" one of them said again sarcastically.

"And your fart was no doubt the sound of thunder," echoed another.

"Rain, rain, come today, so I may slaughter a calf for you. And another with a hump!" somebody else sang.

Some laughed. But the majority were not at all amused, expressing their disgust in wordless noises. They now started talking among themselves.

"You know, there is a grain of truth in what drunkards sometimes say."

"One can say that alcohol gives a person insight into things. Drunkards have a way of seeing things."

"That is very true, because what this drunkard has said is nothing but the truth. Our country is truly as dry as this concrete floor. Our leaders have hearts as cold as that of Pharaoh. Or even colder than those of the colonialists. They cannot hear the cry of the people."

"You have a point there. For one, can you tell me why I was arrested today?"

"And what about me?"

They all forgot about the urine, and they began telling stories of their arrest. The way they talked they might have known one another for years.

One of them was a peasant farmer. He had been arrested for selling milk without a license.

"Just one bottle of milk, my friends! Just when I had bought some candles to take home, here they come with handcuffs: 'Where is your permit?'"

Another had been arrested for stealing food from a restaurant.

"What could I have done? I was famished, my friends."

Yet another was accused of murdering a wealthy landowner who had failed to pay him his wages.

"I hit him with a stick, and he fell down dead. . . but he had really provoked me. Just imagine your wife and children waiting for you to take some flour home and then you walk in empty handed. And it is not as if you are begging. You are only demanding the wages you have worked for."

A fourth had been arrested for vagrancy.

"Have I turned down any job? Just imagine being arrested for vagrancy in your own country!"

Among them was a student who had been arrested for asking the Provincial Commissioner about the running of the country since independence.

"And do you know what I asked him? 'Why do you wear colonial uniforms?' Are they gods so that they may not be questioned? *I say, where is democracy in this country?* The Provincial Commissioner threatened: 'You'll have it rough, you university students. And you, chief, you have failed in your duties, or what is all this about, mere children yelling at adults in this manner?' *So I am here under the notorious Chiefs Act!"*

Another was a teacher who had been arrested and accused of teaching Marxism and communism in school.

"Do you know what they based the allegations on? The fact that I stated that the political and economic systems of countries like the Soviet Union, China, Cuba and many other socialist countries are based on the teachings of Marx and Lenin. I have only one question. If I can't teach the truth, what should I teach, then?"

The seventh man had been accused of having an intention to snatch a bourgeois woman's purse.

"I saw this wealthy woman unrolling a wad of hundred-shilling notes, and thought to myself: That money belongs to us, doesn't it? I'll help her spend it. So I followed her, and when she was about to get into her Mercedes, I. . . But how was I to know that there was a plain-clothes policeman right next to me? They brought me in for being a pickpocket."

The drunkard had been arrested simply for being drunk.

"Can you tell me the logic of that?" he asked. "If I don't drink, what am I supposed to do with my life?"

By now only Matigari and two others present had not yet explained why they had been arrested.

"It is true that our present leaders have no mercy," the peasant farmer added. "First they arrest us for no reason at all; then they bring us to a cell with no toilet facilities. So we end up pissing and shitting on one another!"

"Even if there were toilets," the one accused of theft said, "I would have absolutely nothing to put in them. When was the last time I put a morsel into this belly?"

"And what about me?" asked the 'pickpocket'. "I'm starving!"

"I have often read in newspapers that they do feed people in prisons," the student now said.

"Yes, when the Lord above wills it!" the drunkard exclaimed.

It was then that Matigari remembered that he still had his packed food and a bottle of beer.

"I've a portion of food here, packed for me earlier in the day. I also have a bottle of beer. We can all share the food and have a sip of my beer. That way, we can keep hunger at bay for a while. It is not the quantity that counts but the act of sharing whatever we have. What did we use to sing?

> Great love I saw there,
> Among the women and the children.
> When a bean fell,
> We would share it among ourselves.

"Our people, let us share this bean, and this drop of wine."

Something in Matigari's voice made them listen to him attentively. There was a sad note about it, but it also carried hope and courage. The others now fell silent. His words seemed to remind them of things long forgotten, carrying them back to dreams they had had long before.

"How are we going to see in this darkness?" the 'vagrant' asked.

"Finding your mouth can't really be all that hard," the one accused of murder said.

"A bit of food might fall into the urine," said the 'pickpocket'.

"Or in the vomit," the 'thief' added.

"Then the vomit and piss will be our gravy," the student joked.

"What are you saying?" the 'vagrant' asked in disgust. "Don't you know that you can make me sick?"

"Or make us loose our appetites?" the 'pickpocket' said.

"That's no problem. I can have your share," the 'thief' said.

"Why, are you the ogre in the story who looked after the expectant woman and starved her?" the 'vagrant' asked. "Or are you one of those ogres currently running the country?"

It was the peasant who came out with the answer to their problem.

"I was arrested just as I came from buying candles," he said. "We can light one or two so that we can see while we eat. We don't want to bite off our fingers. The only trouble is that I have no matches."

"I have a box of matches," said the teacher.

They lit two candles. They all peered at each other's faces as if trying to find out who it was that had saved them from hunger. The shadows danced on their faces and on the wall. They all turned their eyes to Matigari.

Matigari took the food, broke it and gave it to them. They started eating. Then he took the bottle of beer, opened it with his teeth, poured a little of it on the floor in libation and gave them to drink and pass round.

When the drunkard's turn came, he leaped to his feet, holding the food in his right hand and the bottle in his left, and started speaking as though he were reading the Bible from the pulpit.

"And when the time for the supper came, he sat at the table together with his disciples. He told them: I want you to share this last supper with me, to remind us that we shall not be able to eat together again unless our kingdom comes. And he took the bread and after breaking it he said: This is my body, which I give to you. Do this unto one another until the Second Coming. He then took the cup, and after blessing it he said: And this cup is a testament of the covenant we entered with one another with our blood. Do this to one another until our kingdom comes, through the will of the people!"

The man stopped speaking. Then he turned to Matigari:

"Tell us the truth. Who are you? Because I have never heard of anyone ever being allowed to carry food or beer into the cell. I have been to prison countless times, and I swear that there's never been a time when they don't give us a thorough search. . . Our shoes, our money, everything is left at the entrance. What, then, happened today? No! I don't believe it. Tell us the word! Give us the good tidings."

He sat down. The men once again turned to Matigari, expecting something extraordinary to happen, for there was a grain of truth in what the drunkard had said. They had all been arrested on that day. But none of their things had been taken away from them. Matigari began speaking, like a father to his children.

"I lived on a farm stolen from me by Settler Williams. I cleared the bush, tilled the soil, sowed the seeds and tended the crop. But what about the harvest? Everything went into Settler Williams' stores, and I the tiller would be left looking for any grain that may have remained in the chaff. Settler Williams yawned because he was well fed. I yawned because I was hungry.

"That was not all. I built the coffee factory and the tea processing industries. You know those fruit-canning industries? I built them too and many others. I did it all with my own hands, yes, with these ten fingers you see here. But who reaped the profits? Settler Williams. And what of me? A cent was flung in my direction. The moment I got my meager wages, who do you think was waiting for me at the gate but Settler Williams's tax collectors? And if I failed to pay? Off to prison I went!

"Don't think that this was all, my friends! These hands of mine built a house. I the builder would sleep on the threshold or I would go begging for a place to lay my head. And all this while Settler Williams occupied the house that I had built! Tell me, is it fair that the tailor should go naked, the builder sleep in the open air and the tiller go hungry?

"I revolted against this scheme of things.

"I took the oath of patriotism and, one early morning, I went to Settler Williams and said: Pack your bags. Go build your own house. You have two hands just like I have. He refused to leave. He ran to the phone and I to the armory. And who do you think it was that jumped on my back, screaming a warning to Settler Williams? None other than John Boy! I escaped through the window and ran up and down slopes. I ran through many valleys and disappeared into the mountains. Settler Williams and John Boy came after me. We spent many years hunting one another in every corner of the land. I first killed John Boy. It was only yesterday that I finally got Williams and stepped on his chest, holding up the weapons of victory. The battle won, I decided to come home and claim my house.

"Our people! Would you believe it? Who do you think I met standing at the gate to my house? John Boy's son, and Settler

Williams's son! So it was Boy, son of Boy, who inherited the keys to my house! They blew the whistle, and the police came for me. Where is the justice in this, my friends?

"Friends, you asked me a question, and I have answered it. That's it. I'm here because, according to them, I don't have the title-deed to my house. But tell me — what title-deed is greater than our sweat and blood? Whom do we turn to, we the patriots, we, Matigari ma Njirũũngi!"

"Matigari ma Njirũũngi?" the two men who had not yet spoken exclaimed together. "Was it you who stopped the police dogs from attacking a woman today?"

The others were startled out of the dreamland to which they had been transported by his story.

"Are you the one of whom Ngarũro wa Kĩrĩro spoke at the factory before the police began breaking workers' limbs?" said one of the two men who had spoken simultaneously.

"Before the police broke people's legs at the factory? When? Today?" some asked, turning in the direction of the person who had come up with this news.

"Haven't you heard how the police beat the workers at the factory?"

"You too! Tell us your story."

They sat up, their eyes now keenly glued to the man as he spoke.

"I'm a worker," he began his tale. "I have worked with the company for ages, and the words Matigari has just spoken are absolutely true. I have been a servant to those machines all my life. Look at how the machines have sapped me of all strength. What is left of me? Just bones. My skin withered even as I kept on assuring myself: A fortune for him who works hard finally comes; a person who endures, finally overcomes. What can I now expect when I retire? Just a clock as a thank-you for long and loyal service. My fortune? Old age without a pension. Do you know something else? I spent all these years opposed to strikes. I kept on saying: If I go on strike and lose my job, what will my children eat tomorrow? But look at me. Here I am in prison for no reason whatsoever. What went wrong? Let me tell you.

"Even today, this very day, I was walking along the road on my way home. I said to myself: Let me leave the strike to the foolish brave, listening to the experts like Ngarũro wa Kĩrĩro. A man my age stopped and asked me: "Have you heard the news?" What news, other than the news of the strike? I said. And he answered me: "No, that is not what I am talking about. I am talking about the patriots who went away. Listen! They have come back. Our children will come back." What has happened? I asked him. "Can you believe this! He is a dwarf of a man. What did I say? A dwarf? When this dwarf stood up, wearing a feathered hat and a leopard-skin coat over his shoulder, he was transformed into a giant. I say again, a giant! He stood tall and strong and told the dog police: I am Matigari ma Njiruũngi, and I warn you. Leave that woman alone! How can I describe it? His voice was like thunder. The dogs stopped with their tails in mid-air. Have you ever heard of such a thing?" Just as this man was telling me all this, I saw flames burst out in the factory compound and I knew that they were burning the effigies of Boy and Williams. The workers cheered. Then I heard Ngarũro wa Kĩrĩro's voice carried on the wind by the loudspeaker. Mark you, I only caught the last words: "Foreign exploiters and their local servants must now pack up their bags and go. The patriots, Matigari ma Njiruũngi, are back, and the workers agree with Matigari's call. He who sows must be the one who reaps! We refuse to be the pot that cooks but never eats the food!"

"Ngarũro wa Kĩrĩro's words made me happy. When I saw the effigies of Boy and Williams burning in the workers' fire, I felt more than happy. I felt like weeping with joy. You see, I have worked in the factory for many years. I have seen French, German, Canadian and Italian directors come and go, but I have never seen worse directors than Boy and Williams. Boy is the worst of the two. He is like those dogs that are said to bark louder than their masters. He is really rude and arrogant. He claims that his shit never smells! Tell me, who wouldn't rejoice at seeing the likes of those two burning eternally in hell? Our God will come back, yes, the God of us workers will surely come back.

"Just as I was thinking about Boy and Williams, I saw riot and mounted police encircle us. I abandoned the man of my age and his stories and I fled as fast as these old little legs could carry me. You might think that this is the first time that I have run away from a workers' strike. No. I am a veteran at running away from the scene of a workers' strike. The workers were fleeing in every direction. The police and the soldiers followed in hot pursuit. Our eyes were smarting from the tear-gas they kept firing at us. By the time I had taken three, four steps, a hand gripped me. "Got you! Why are you running away?" I was thrown into a Land-Rover unceremoniously. And that's how I came to be here. A lot of people were locked up in the factory, as there weren't enough cells in the police stations around. The others with whom I was arrested were taken to another police station, but there was no room for me, so they brought me here. That is why I ask you: Are you really Matigari ma Njirũũngi?"

"Yes, you have said it," Matigari answered. Then he asked the worker, "Do you know if Ngarũro wa Kĩrĩro has been arrested?"

"I don't know, but I heard the police say that they were looking for him everywhere. He somehow managed to slip through their fingers," the worker said.

"Where have truth and justice gone to in this country?" Matigari said as he remembered Ngarũro wa Kĩrĩro and how he had helped him to his feet earlier in the day.

"I will unravel that riddle for you," the man accused of theft told him. "Don't think that I am slighting or insulting you. But if you continue asking questions of that kind, you will find yourself in a mental hospital or in a pit of everlasting darkness."

"A pit deeper than the one we are already in?" the drunkard asked. Then he turned to Matigari. "From today you will be known as the seeker of truth and justice. Don't take it too hard! The son of God was baptized by John the Baptist. That is why I have taken the liberty of baptizing you."

"Truth seeking justice?" the peasant mused on the drunkard's words slowly. "Justice seeking truth! The Seeker of Truth and Justice!"

"Yes, true justice is mightier than the sword. Truth once convinced an archer to loosen the bow he had drawn against his enemy," the drunkard added.

"But don't you know that the government has a Ministry of Truth and Justice?" the student reminded them.

"The Minister for Truth and Justice is actually coming to pay a visit to the factory tomorrow," the worker said.

"So the Seeker of Truth and Justice can ask the minister for the job of seeking truth and justice," the student said in jest. "This is the first commandment: You shall not mention the name of truth and justice in vain."

"Let me be prudent and keep my mouth shut!" the 'thief' said. "Is this one here not a teacher? What has he just said? He was brought here for talking too much. And what of this student? The same. So I bid my lips be silent."

"Tell us why you are here," the student asked him.

"Hunger. Hunger brought me here," the 'thief' answered.

They all laughed. The man who had not yet spoken now cleared his throat. Addressing Matigari, he said, "May I ask you a question? You say that you returned from the forest this morning. Where are your weapons? Where did you leave them? Or did you have them on you when you were arrested?"

"You may ask me as many questions as you like. I say questions are the gateway to wisdom and knowledge. Show me a person who does not ask questions, and I will show you an idiot. Well, I buried my weapons under the roots of a *mũgumo* tree. I then girded myself with a belt of peace, saying: The flag now belongs to the blacks. So from now onwards, let justice and truth break down all the bows drawn in war; let truth and justice settle all the disputes amongst us black people. Let truth and justice rule the world."

"But how do we know that you are really Matigari ma Njirũũngi? How can we identify you? Where is the sign?"

"The sign?. . . Oh, that the reign of justice may begin now. . .Let it be now, for if not. . ." Matigari talked as if the man had asked him about the signs of the Second Coming. "Listen. . . I don't need anything to prove who I am. I don't need signs or miracles. My actions will be my trumpet and they shall speak for me, For I will remove this belt of peace and I will wear another, decorated with bullets instead of beads. Yes, I will wear a gun around my waist and carry my AK47 over my shoulder; and I shall stand on top of the highest mountain and tell it to all the people: Open your eyes and see what I have seen. . . Open your ears and hear what I have heard. Let the will of the people be done! Our kingdom come as once decreed by the Iregi revolutionaries: The land belongs to the tiller and not to parasites and foreigners! Therefore the tiller must reap what he sows; the builder must have shelter; the tailor must have clothes to wear; the producer must have the power over his produce!"

"What you have said is true," the peasant said, "Why shouldn't we peasants eat properly? Why should the builder sleep outside? Why should the tailor walk about in rags?"

"What do you plan to do now?" the other continued, questioning Matigari. "If Boy and Williams don't give you back your house, what are you going to do?"

"Listen to me," the 'murderer' told Matigari, "What were we told here just now? A prudent person keeps their mouth shut, I had better repeat it to you because a leader who does not accept advice is no leader. The forest in the heart is never cleared of all the wood. One carefully selects what to cut and what to leave. I do not know you, and you do not know me. There are a lot of police informers in the country. Wherever you find twelve people gathered, one of them will always be an informer, a traitor. I tell you this: If your name was mentioned at the workers' meeting, then the authorities must be looking for you."

"They are looking for a giant of a man," the student said, laughter welling up in his throat. But it died as quickly as it rose.

The 'murderer' and the man who had been asking questions had jumped to their feet, and as quick as lightning each had taken out a switchblade.

"Are you calling me a traitor?" the man said to the 'murderer'.

"Do informers walk about with signs on their foreheads proclaiming: Look, I'm an informer?" the 'murderer' replied. "Any one of us here could be a police informer."

They made as if they were going to stab at each other, their knives shining in the candle-light.

"Put your knives away!" Matigari ordered them in a powerful voice. "How dare you draw your knives at each other? Aren't you already in enough trouble?"

They put away their knives. Then the student said, "We're only eleven here, so there can't be an informer among us."

Matigari continued with his answer as though nothing had taken place.

"You want to know what I plan to do? I'll tell you, for I have nothing to hide. I have come back to the people girded with a belt of peace. A farmer whose seeds have not germinated does not give up planting. A person who seeks justice never tires of the search until he finds it. Truth never dies, therefore, truth will reign in the end, even if it does not reign today. My house is my house. I am only after what I have built with my own hands. Tomorrow belongs to me. I invite you all to my house the day after tomorrow. Come to a feast and celebrate our homecoming!"

"Do you really think that you will be out of this place that soon?" the 'vagrant' asked. "Getting into gaol is easy, but getting out is always a hard job. I'm sure that you will still be here tomorrow, and even the day after."

"If you had collided with anybody else but the master and his servant, it would have been much better," the worker said. "I should know. That inseparable pair have been oppressing us all this time. Every worker knows that Robert Williams and John Boy are like twins born out of the womb of the same ogre. And do you know something else? The whole police force is in the hands of these two. So are all the law courts. So I think that you will be very lucky to leave this prison soon. You should brace yourself for a long spell here, because, as the saying goes, gaols were built for men."

"And women too!" another added.

"And the children."

"Only Gabriel the angel of God can get you out of here. Amen," the drunkard said.

Hardly had he finished the sentence, before they heard footsteps and the sound of keys jingling in the dark. They quickly blew out the candles and remained dead silent, huddled together. The door creaked. Why should a policeman walk stealthily without switching on the lights? An eeriness crept over them. The creaking sounds drew nearer. They remained a little scared, prepared for the worst. Then the heard a faint voice.

"Come out quietly. Don't make any noise, and don't look back! When you get to the road, you Matigari should wait by the clinic. The rest of you must continue walking without looking back!"

They crept out slowly, one after the other, groping along the prison walls. The doors were open. There was nobody at the reception desk. This must be a dream!

Or perhaps a miracle. Being let out of prison by an invisible person? Yet even as they headed towards the main road, most of them were wondering: Who *was* Matigari ma Njirũũngi, a person who could make prison walls open?

From that night, Matigari's fame spread over all the country. He became a legend. He became a dream. Still the question remained: Who *was* Matigari ma Njirũũngi?

❖

PART TWO

Macaria ma na Kĩhooto

❖

Seeker of Truth and Justice

1

When the children woke up the next day, they found Mũriũki sleeping in his Mercedes-Benz. They woke him up and crowded around him.

"When did you come back?"

"At night."

"Tell us. Tell us about the man. . . Tell us about Matigari ma Njirũũngi."

The story of how Matigari had saved Gũthera from the police dog had already reached them. They had heard how the police had shaken with fear in front of Matigari. The children felt guilty. It was the same police who for many years had harassed them. Why did we attack such a good man? they asked themselves. Where can we find Mũriũki so that he can tell us about that man? That is why they were now pleased to see Mũriũki.

Mũriũki added salt to his story. Their thoughts grew wings: Is it true that he was arrested? Is it true that the prison doors opened mysteriously? Do you think they will announce it on the radio?

One of the boys ran to fetch the radio he had found in the garbage yard. The children had agreed that the radio would be communal property, so they could all listen to the news of the country and the world. They had paid compensation to the boy who had found it. They took the radio everywhere they went.

Now they gathered around to hear anything, any news, about Matigari ma Njirũũngi.

This is the Voice of Truth. . . His Excellency Ole Excellence yesterday received a donation of fifty thousand shillings from businessmen (browns blacks and whites) who paid him a visit at his home. The donation is for the presidential fund for disabled children. The leader of the delegation congratulated His Excellency Ole Excellence for stamping out a mutiny which was intended to disrupt peace and stability in the country. . .

Two university lecturers appeared in court yesterday charged with possessing books on Karl Marx and V. Lenin published in China. All books about the liberation of peasants and workers, particularly those published in China, have been banned since independence. . .

*

Five university students were arrested yesterday for taking part in a demonstration outside the British and United States Embassies. The students were protesting against Western aid to the apartheid regime. All demonstrations were banned in the country by a presidential decree. . .

*

Reports from Johannesburg, South Africa, say that the ANC freedom fighters are responsible for the explosion of a time bomb in a hotel frequented by whites. The whites are said to fear the unity of the SWAPO and ANC guerrillas. . .

*

The USA and the Soviet Union have made much progress in their preparations for voyages to Mars and other planets. Reports reaching us. . .

*

And now for the local news. Reports say that the police yesterday dispersed a workers' meeting at the Anglo-American Leather and Plastic Works where effigies of the two directors, Robert Williams and John Boy, were burned. The police used tear-gas. A number of workers were arrested. The Minister for Truth and Justice will be visiting the factory to settle the dispute in justice and truth.

*

This is the Voice of Truth. Police reports say that a policeman fainted when he found out that some prisoners he had carefully locked in a cell had escaped. The most surprising thing was that the lock on the door of the cell was intact. The bars on the windows had not been tampered with whatsoever. The policeman still had the bunch of keys in his pocket. Police investigations are still being carried out.

Now the sports news. Horse-racing, motor rallying, golf and athletics. . .

*

"Switch it off. It is unbelievable!" the children exclaimed.

"Mūriūki, tell us! Who is Matigari ma Njirūūngi?"

The children spread the news. They took it to the people, who were in any case thirsty for such a story.

For people found here something dramatic, something that livened up their otherwise drab lives. What amazing news! How could prison doors open by themselves? Who was Matigari ma Njirūūngi? The people of Trampville composed a song for Matigari ma Njirūūngi:

> Show me the way to a man
> Whose name is Matigari ma Njirūūngi,
> Who stamps his feet to the rhythm of bells.
> And the bullets jingle.
> And the bullets jingle.

2

There was no sunshine. There was no rain. It was neither warm nor cold. A dull day.

3

He went to many market-places in search of truth and justice. People stood in groups talking about the strange events that had taken place in the country.

"What events?"

"Haven't you heard?"

"Heard what?"

"This strange news?"

"If I had heard it, would I be asking you to tell me about it?"

"Those who went have come back!"

"Which ones?"

"Must you really have everything spelled out? Can't you guess who Matigari ma Njirūūngi are?"

"But those are fairy-tales surely? Are they still living?"

"Rumor has it that they have come back with flaming swords in their hands!"

"Flaming swords?"

"Yes! To claim the products of our labor."

"Just a minute! Say that again."

"The country has its patriots."

"Have you actually seen him, or are these rumors?"

Everyone anxiously waited for an answer. Who was Matigari? What did he look like?

At that moment, Matigari appeared before them. He stood about two paces away from them and greeted them.

They all turned towards him.

"My friends! Can you tell me where a person could find truth and justice in this country?"

They looked at him disapprovingly. Some made wordless noises of disapproval. They turned their eyes away from him.

"What is this man asking? Let's first hear stories about Matigari ma Njirũũngi! Have you set eyes upon him? What does he look like? How big is he?"

4

He went to shopping centers. Everywhere, shopkeepers and their customers crowded the counters and the entrances. . .

"The children were the first to see him."

"The children? Did he reveal himself to them? A child and a king are one and the same thing. But children will always be children!"

"Why? What did they do?"

"They threw stones at him."

"Stones? Didn't they know who he was?"

"No."

"These modern children. They ought to be ashamed of themselves, throwing stones at an elderly man. Suppose they hit him in the eyes?"

"That is the amazing thing. Not even one stone touched him."

"What?"

"When the stones reached him, they changed into doves."

"Doves?"

"Yes! You think that this is a small matter, don't you?"

"The children were scared. Then some other people came by

and they asked the children: Why are you stoning the old man? But he said: Let the children come to me. Yet the children were afraid, and they began to run away. Only one boy went to him."

"Let me say a word. It is not good to look down upon a person on account of how he dresses or how he looks. A hero cannot be judged by his size. I'd be happy if I could see him with my own eyes, this very minute, so that I can shake his hand. . ."

Matigari came up to them and stood on the verandah.

"Kindly tell me this, my friends. Where can one find truth and justice in this society?"

They fell silent and just stared at the stranger as if he had struck the wrong chord of a popular melody. Then they started talking to one another and complaining about the man who had spoiled their song.

"What on earth is he talking about?"

"Yes, how can he cut us short in the middle of such an interesting story to ask such nonsensical questions?"

"Why can't he go to the Voice of Truth?"

"Or to the Ministry of Truth and Justice?"

"Leave him alone. He's probably a drunkard."

"Yes, tell us more about Matigari ma Njirũũngi. Where did he go when he left the children? Where did he go with the boy?"

5

He visited many eating places. People were so absorbed in the extraordinary tales of Matigari that they often forgot to drink their tea or eat their food. They just sat and listened.

"It was Ngarũro wa Kĩrĩro who first discovered who he was."

"Ngarũro wa Kĩrĩro? I've always said that Ngarũro has a way of seeing into things."

"He's one of those with natural wisdom."

"Hurray! Up with Ngarũro wa Kĩrĩro!"

"You know when Ngarũro wa Kĩrĩro addressed the meeting yesterday? Everybody's heart was beating as if they were ready to take up arms there and then. His words were so encouraging that even if one had sat on fire one would not have noticed it: Cast your fears away, for we are not alone! Our patriots are still living. That is what he said to them. He also told them how Matigari had appeared to him, and how he had spoken in parables and proverbs, saying: The products of our labor should go back to us who produce the wealth of this country. He said that imperialists and their overseers should pack their bags, because the owners of the country are back. Ngarũro wa Kĩrĩro asked them: Who are the owners of the country? And the crowd answered in one voice: We are! We, the workers and peasants! That is when they started burning the effigies of Robert Williams and John Boy! Then came the police and the soldiers. The people were trapped between the police on the one side and the factory walls on the other. The factory was converted into a prison."

"What else did Ngarũro wa Kĩrĩro say about Matigari ma Njirũũngi? What message did he bring from Matigari ma Njirũũngi?"

"What greater message do you want? He said that the products of toil should go to those who toil."

"What Matigari said is nothing but the real truth and justice. How can the tiller go on working for the benefit of those-who-reap-where-they-never-sowed? Yesterday it was the whites. Today they have been joined by some blacks."

Matigari walked into the restaurant and sat down. He ordered a cup of tea.

"My friends! Tell me where in this country one can find truth and justice."

People raised their heads. Who was this who interrupted the sweet tale about Matigari?

"Who are you, Mr. Seeker of Truth and Justice?"

"That is who I am," Matigari answered.

"We were just talking about something that might interest you. Let me give you a bit of advice. If you want to hear truth and justice, or just plain truth, go and look for the prophet who has come to our land."

"Who is he? Where can I find him?"

"He is called Matigari ma Njirũũngi. Ngarũro wa Kĩrĩro knows him. Ngarũro was actually with him yesterday."

6

He went to the crossroads. Women returning from the river would put down their cans, pots and barrels so as to exchange stories about Matigari.

"He is actually a tiny, ordinary-looking man."

"Is he old?"

"In appearance, yes."

"So he is one of those with a small build?"

"Just wait till you hear the whole story! You see, the entire population from the market-place had gathered around the spot, just to watch the police set a dog on a woman."

"How long is this police oppression going to go on for? In the past, before the whites brought imperialism here, did we ever have police and soldiers? Never! Were there any prisons? No! Was there as much crime as there is today? No! We used to rule ourselves, didn't we?"

"Let us first hear the story in full."

"The girl was screaming with fright. But people just stood as if their very backbones were made of fear. Or as if their veins and arteries had fear flowing in them instead of blood."

"Fear. Too much fear breeds misery in the land."

"Those were the same words that Matigari told them."

"The same tiny man? So he has something to say for himself?"

"Did you say tiny? The man is a giant. He could easily touch the sky!"

"What?"

"Yes! A giant who could almost touch the sky above."

"Tell us more!"

"What can I tell you that you haven't already heard? When he stood up, the grey of his hair and the wrinkles on his face seemed to disappear. His shadow stretched and stretched on the ground. "Don't touch her. This is a woman of the land!" he told the police. "Don't you as much as lay a finger on her."

"Oh, bless our patriots! Wasn't he afraid?"

"Why should he fear? Freedom fighters are alien to the word 'fear.' Can you imagine! He repeated his warnings: Whoever dares touch that woman will know who we really are, we, Matigari Ma Njirũũngi!"

"Good God! Who would ever have thought that fear would

one day disappear from our land? That a day would come when people would no longer walk with their heads bent in fear? That a day would come when people need not whisper when discussing their lives?"

"Yes, let's hope for that day! Yesterday we caught a glimpse of it. The dogs and the policeman just dropped their tails between their legs and took off."

"But didn't they have guns?"

"Even if you were the one who had a gun, you would have slunk away in a similar fashion. His voice alone was like thunder and his eyes like fire! Smoke was gushing out of his nose, mouth and ears!"

"Such wonders! I wish I had been there to see him and shake his hand, or sing him a song like the one the people of Trampville composed!

> Show me the way to a man
> Whose name is Matigari ma Njirũũngi,
> Who stamps his feet to the rhythm of bells.
> And the bullets jingle.
> And the bullets jingle.

"You mean sing while holding him close to your breasts," one of them said slyly.

They laughed.

Just then Matigari stopped on the other side of the road and greeted them,

"Our people! Where can one find truth and justice in this country?"

"What? What is he asking now? Let me be off."

"Me too."

"And me."

"I'll go now. . ."

They all picked up their water barrels and went away.

7

He wandered across the farmlands. . .

"Is it true that John Boy Junior was so scared that he wet himself?"

"He did worse than that!"

"R-e-a-l-l-y? A rich tyrant like him to actually piss and shit on himself?"

"You would do the same if you found yourself caught in the same situation he was. Walking about showing off with other people's property! Yes, suppose the owner turns up and asks you: What are you doing with my things? Wouldn't you piss and shit?"

"Is it true that Robert Williams was also there?"

"Yes. A servant and his boss are inseparable. Matigari spotted them immediately. They were both on horseback. *Clopity-clop, clopity-clop, clopity-clop.* As they approached the gates, their horses stopped abruptly. They tried to spur them on, but they just reared, neighing in fright."

"Like the horse that once saw the angel of the Lord standing on the road?"

"That wasn't a horse; it was an ass!"

"Arguments later — let's first listen to the story!"

"Then they saw him standing in the middle of the road, with his hand on his hip. In his other hand, he held a flaming sword."

"Did you hear that! A flaming sword!"

"Then he said to them: You breed of parasites! Give back the keys to these houses and these lands which you took away from the people!"

"Say that again! What did he actually say? That the whole clan of white and black parasites must *do what?*"

"Give the stolen wealth back to the owners!"

"That is good. Serves the imperialists and their servants right! They have really milked us dry. Yesterday it was the imperialist settlers and their servants. Today it is the same. On the plantations, in the factories, it is still the same duo. The imperialist and his servant. When will we, the family of those who toil, come to our own?"

"That is what Matigari ma Njirũũngi was saying: Imperialist foreigners and their servants out! This country has its owners."

"He really told them the truth."

"Absolutely."

"Oh, yes. The real hidden truth."

"Yes, I have always said it: Where will these sell-outs go when the freedom fighters return, roaring like lions to the tune, "Patriots here! Sell-outs against the wall!?""

"It is really true, that things will not remain the way they are today. For how can the present conditions continue when foreigners, be they from Europe or America, can always get places on which to pitch their tents? Tents in which to hide their military gadgets? Tents in which to store the wealth stolen from us! And when their black overseers are busy taming the entire population with honeyed tongues or silencing them with police boots!"

"You too have spoken another of Matigari's truths. Because even after they had arrested him, he just said to them: Don't rejoice just because you have thrown me in this hell. You will see me again after only three days."

"Tell us more. . . Why can't this Matigari ma Njirũũngi come here to the farmlands? If he came, I would tell him: Keep it up. . ."

They saw a man standing by a tea-bush.

"Tell me, my people! Where can one find truth and justice in this country?"

"Who is this asking such difficult questions?"

"Who are you?"

"Just a seeker of truth and justice," Matigari answered.

"Go back the way you've come and look for a man called Matigari ma Njirũũngi. He is the one who now beats the rhythm to the tune, 'truth and again truth.' If you find him, ask him this: Since justice is mightier than force, where does its force come from?"

8

He went to the law courts. Those awaiting trial were all talking about Matigari.

"Why can't he come here, loosen these fetters and set me free?"

"Are you sure that that is what really happened?"

"Didn't you read the papers?"

"These newspaper people never sleep, do they? How did they get to know something that happened only last night?"

"The newspapers say it wasn't all that late. There was only one policeman on duty, as most of the others had gone to the factory to beat and guard the striking workers. The only other policeman was in the camp, cooking *ugali*. According to the paper, he swears that he actually locked up the prisoners in one cell, switched off the lights, pocketed the keys and went to his desk. But when he later returned to check the cell, he found it bare. The lock was still intact. It had not been broken at all, or tampered with in any way. Our policeman just fell on the floor, pleading with God in heaven: Have mercy on me, O Lord, for I am a sinner before thee! I beg you to tell me if it is thy hand which has set them free, as you once did long ago in the case of Paul and the Capernaum prison!"

"But this newspaper has omitted a lot of details. People are saying that there was thunder and lightning for about one hour! Everyone thought that it was going to rain, but not even a drop of rain fell. Then, all at once, the thunder and the lightning stopped."

"So perhaps it was the thunder that loosened the door?"

"But how do you explain the fact that the lock was still intact? And that there was not a single crack in the door? And that all the walls were in place?"

"This is truly amazing. And yet skeptics still don't believe in miracles! What more proof do they need?"

"You know, some people read about all the miracles done by Moses and they think that all those are just biblical myths."

"Of course miracles happen. The other day I saw a man taking a pigeon out of his hat and a five-shilling note from the nose of a three-year-old —"

"Stop these pigeon lies! The only thing I'd like to know is, who is Matigari?"

"Don't you know that the Bible says he shall come back again?"

"Do you mean to say he's the One prophesied about? The Son of Man?"

"Why not? Let's count. Where is the oldest church in the world? In Ethiopia, Africa. When he was a baby, where did he flee to? Egypt, Africa. What has happened before can happen again. If he appeared before me now, I would hold his hand, kneel down before him and tell him: Lord, let us who were left behind now lead the way. I would then sit on his right-hand side and tell him: Look at these white and black parasites. Look! See the Boys and the Williamses coming to you. Please send them away and have them thrown into the everlasting fire you made for the likes of imperialists and their overseers. For you were hungry, but they gave you no food; you were thirsty, and they gave you no water; you were naked, but they clothed you not. You were sick, but they never visited you. And when you were in gaol, they did not visit you. Lord, don't listen to their prayers! Do you hear their hypocritical questions? They have the audacity to ask: Lord, when saw we thee hungry and thirsty and naked and sick and in prison, and did not minister unto thee? Tell them the truth, Lord. Show them your justice! Answer them: Verily I say unto you, in as much as ye did it not to one of the least of these in this court room, ye did it not to me. Send them away, Lord. Hey, you sinners over there! Didn't you hear what the Lord said to you? Go away, you scum of the earth who are even prepared to sell away the sovereignty of your country! Go away!"

Matigari just arrived, only to find a man speaking and pointing a finger in his direction. "Go away!"

He interrupted their conversation with his greetings:

"Tell me, my people! Where in this country can one find truth and justice?"

"What did you say?"

"I am looking for truth and justice in this country!"

"You really brought yourself to these courts in search of truth and justice?"

"But is this not where the judges and lawyers are to be found?" Matigari asked.

"Shall I answer your question with the real truth?"

"Yes. I am looking for no justice other than the justice which has its roots in truth."

"Let me give you a bit of advice, then. Go get a rope and hang yourself immediately. . . for your kind of questions will lead you to the grave. . ."

He went away, shocked.

9

His thoughts weighed down on him. He went to a kiosk across the road and he asked for a cup of black tea. He asked the kiosk keeper, "Where can one find truth and justice here?"

The kiosk keeper looked at him as though he did not understand the question.

"We small traders don't know or care about such things. If you were asking me where you and I could go and buy a sack of sugar cheaply, so that we could earn a cent or two in profit, I would know how to answer you. As for the rest let me put on the Voice of Truth for you!"

. . . Space. . . space shuttles. . . United States. . . Soviet Union. . . EEC. . . China. . . Japan. . . nuclear bombs. . . ANC. . . PLO. . . SWAPO. . . Nicaragua. . . El Salvador. . . His Excellency Ole Excellence. . . Ole Excellence there. . . Ole Excellence all over. . .Those were the news headlines from the Voice of Truth. . . Here is the full news bulletin. . .

*

A special announcement. . . The government has announced that the public should be wary of some terrorists who are walking about the country claiming to be Matigari ma Njiru-u-ngi. The government has said that all freedom fighters returned from the mountains the day the independence flag was hoisted. We are all freedom fighters. Those spreading such rumors are out to disrupt the peace, like the soldiers who mutinied. . .

*

Two university students who appeared in court yesterday on charges of possessing seditious documents were detained without trial after the government entered a non-prosequitur. *. .*

Five other students arrested yesterday on charges of illegal demonstration in protest against United States and Western European support of the South African apartheid regime were each given a five-year sentence. They were led away shouting: Victory to the people!

The students who wanted to form a national union of students have been urged to stop provoking the government. . . There is only one party in the country. Why do the students want another party? His Excellency Ole Excellence said that the students should all be satisfied with one party the ruling party.

*

The minister for Truth and Justice began his tour of rural areas today. He will be visiting the Anglo-American Leather and Plastic Factory. He will be addressing the directors and the workers. The factory was the scene of a clash between the police and the workers yesterday. The workers who were on strike burned effigies of the directors. Reports say that if the police had not intervened the workers would have carried out what the police suspected to be deliberate acts of sabotage and arson. Such actions would have done a lot of harm to the economy.

*

Special announcement. . . special announcement. . . Government spokesman has announced that people should not heed the rumors spreading in the country that the Angel Gabriel let some prisoners out of their cell and that one of the prisoners was Jesus Christ. There is no truth whatsoever in these rumors about Jesus or Gabriel returning. The government will not hesitate to clamp down on any religion claiming that Christ has come back. The government will not hesitate to withdraw licenses from mata-tus* which allow such rumors to continue. Those are false Christs and false Gabriels. There is no way that Jesus could return without first going to pay a courtesy call on His Excellency Ole Excellence. Members of the public are urged to report anyone claiming to be Jesus or Gabriel to the nearest police station. . .

10

The true seeker of truth never loses hope. The true seeker of real justice never tires. A farmer does not stop planting seeds just because of the failure of one crop. Success is born of trying and trying again. Truth must seek justice. Justice must seek the truth. When justice triumphs, truth will reign on earth.

11

He travelled on foot. He rode on donkey carts. He got lifts on bicycles. He traveled in *matatus,** buses and lorries. He travelled by train. He went to all the places where people were likely to gather. And in all the places he asked the one question: How and where can a person girded with a belt of peace find Truth and Justice?

And since their heads were so full of the rumors that had spread over the whole country like wildfire over dry plains, they just stared at him as though they did not understand what it was he was asking. They would turn their attention to the much more exciting tale about Jesus, Gabriel, Matigari ma Njirũũngi, about prison doors opening mysteriously, about the escape of the prisoners, such stories. . .

And the day remained dull. Not hot, not cold. No sunshine, no rain. Just lukewarm.

And now he was saddened because he bore a burden alone in his heart. It was a heavy burden of many unanswered questions, which he turned in his mind alone. What frightened him was the feeling that he was perhaps the only one preoccupied with what was happening in the country - indeed, as if he was all alone in the entire country. But what bothered him even more was Gũthera's story. Whenever he recalled how she had saved him, he would ask himself a lot of questions. If. . . If. . . If. . . If. . . If what? The line that divided truth from lies, good from bad, purity from evil, where was it? What was the difference between right and wrong? Who was the evil one? Was it the one who led another into sin, or the one who actually sinned? Who was the bad one? The one who drove another into bad ways, or the one caught carrying out the evil? Long before, children had sung to the five different fingers of their hands:

First little finger said: Let's go!
And the second asked: Where to?

Matatu: originally an unlicensed 'pirate' taxi. *Matatus* are now a recognized form of public transport, comprising cars or converted pick-ups, usually crammed with passengers, who often engage in lively debate, exchanging news, stories and gossip.

The third said: To steal?
And the index: Suppose we are caught.
The thumb said: Count me out!

What was to be righted first? The condition which led people to sin, or the souls of the people who sinned?

Where were truth and justice in life?

He felt so lonely. Thoughts of saving himself only and forgetting all the rest crept into him and weakened his resolve. He left behind the paths walked by the people. He went into the wilderness.

12

He looked for truth and justice in the grass and in the bushes. He searched among the thorns, in the shrubs, the ditches and the molehills, and in birds' nests. He searched for them in the whole of nature. He was like one deranged. And all the while his heart beat: A farmer does not stop sowing just because one crop has failed. The seeker of justice does not stop searching until he finds it. Truth never dies. Justice is mightier than strength. Tell me: Where on this earth can one find truth and justice?

He came across some shepherds on the plains. As he drew near to where they were, he saw that they had two radios; a Sanyo and a Philips model. They were on full blast. They were both tuned to the same channel.

This is the Voice of Truth. . . His Excellency. . .

Radios bleeping in the wilderness. The Voice of Truth had become the herdsman's flute that lulled the herds to sleep. He ran away, but not bound for anywhere. The announcer's voice seemed to chase him across the plains. . .

He came across an old woman collecting rubbish outside her shelter in the wilderness. Her hair was knotted. A comb had not passed through it for a fair while. Matigari walked up to her and asked for some water to drink.

"If you continue like this, you'll end up like me — picking leaves and talking to yourself!" she shouted, although Matigari was standing close to her. "What are you looking for in the wilderness?"

"Truth and justice," Matigari answered.

The woman laughed, a mixture of genuine pity and sarcasm, and handed him water to drink.

"My dear wanderer, you cannot find answers to your questions here where nobody lives. Truth and justice are to be found in people's actions. Right and wrong are embedded in what people do. But even among the people, you still have a problem in finding the answers to your questions. And do you know why? Let me whisper this in your ear. Come closer. It is fear. There is too much fear in this country. How does the saying go? Too much fear breeds misery in the land. Leave me in peace. Go! Go to the wise men, those who know how to read the stars."

"Do they still exist?" he asked. "I thought that the shepherds were the wise men, for they have always studied the stars. The stars used to guide them in the wilderness. It was during their wanderings that they composed songs containing all the wisdom gathered from the stars! But weren't they the ones I now found, bending over their radios, listening to the Voice of Truth to get guidance across the wilderness? They no longer study the stars. They study the Voice of Truth. . ."

"Go then and plead with those who study books. Books are the modern stars. Those who study them are the wise men of today. Why do you think they are being harassed so much? Why do you think they are being asked to sing only to the tune of the one person? That they must only echo the one man, singing "his master's voice?" Happy are they who suffer in search of truth, for their minds and hearts are free, and they hold the key to the future. But it does not mean that they have all seen the same light at the same time, or that they have all been redeemed of fear! Tell me this: Isn't it possible for one to find at least one or two among them who have been freed of fear and can untie the knot and reveal what's hidden? Here, take some food. . . Over there, you will find the road. . . Farewell. . . Let me continue sweeping this dirt that has so quickly accumulated in our country!"

The woman continued sweeping and collecting rubbish.

Matigari set off again, many questions still troubling him. Why didn't I think of it before? The student I met yesterday and the teacher, were they not arrested for seeking the truth? Let me start my search from scratch. Looking for truth and justice is truly a hard job. Yet, no matter how tired I become, I will never stop searching. How can I let John Boy, a messenger, and the settler — the whole breed of parasites — grab the house that I built with my own hands? How can I let him keep the home for which I shed my blood? How can my wealth remain in the hands of the whole breed of those-who-reap-where-they-never-sowed and their black messengers?

Most of all, he was inspired by the depth of Gũthera's and Mũriũki's commitment to him. He thought of Gũthera. He thought of Mũriũki. Their agony had become his agony; their suffering, his suffering.

As he recalled how Gũthera had given herself as a sacrificial lamb for his salvation, a sharp pain stabbed his heart, and he felt tears sting his eyelids. He asked himself over and over again: In what corner of the earth, this earth, are truth and justice hiding? For how long shall my children continue wandering, homeless, naked and hungry, over this earth? And who shall wipe away the tears from the faces of all the women dispossessed on this earth?

No! In nature and in history there was a mysterious knot, Matigari felt strongly. He had to find someone who could untie the knot, somebody who could reveal the secret of the Universe.

13

It would have been better if it had clearly rained or clearly shone. Better any of that than this uncertain weather. Yes, better if it were hot or cold, rather than lukewarm like this.

He went in search of the wise who taught and studied modern stars.

14

The student had locked himself in his study. When he saw Matigari, he trembled so much so that the book he was holding fell on the floor. He did not even offer him a seat.

"What is it? What is it?" the student asked in a frightened voice.

Matigari paused for a while. Could this be the very same student with whom he had shared the police cell? What had happened to his light-hearted jokes and manner? Where had all his courage gone to? Matigari explained the purpose of his visit.

"I have traveled the length and breadth of this country looking for truth and justice. I met a woman in the plains who said to me: Why have you left behind the students of modern stars? That reminded me of you — that you and I were together yesterday. So I said to myself: Yes, wasn't the student arrested because of searching for the truth? Let me start my search afresh. One must never scorn a grain of sand or a drop of rain. That is why I am here. Open those books that you are studying, and tell me: Where can a person girded with a belt of peace find truth and justice in this country?"

"Listen," said the student, still trembling and full of fear, "these days are not like the days we used to know, our yesterdays. Did you hear the radio announcement today? Five university students were sentenced to five years' imprisonment in a maximum-security prison. And that is not all. . ." The student hesitated. He felt sad. As he spoke, his voice was full of tears of many years. "When did we part? Was it only yesterday evening? Or was it the day before? Anyway, it doesn't matter. Yesterday, the day before, years ago, it has been the same story. I rushed to the university to hide among the other students. I found that they had called a prayer-meeting at the church to pray for those who had been arrested. They also wanted to pray for peace and love in the country. Oh! Oh! Do you know what we went through? The same fate as was meted out to the workers. As we were kneeling down, our eyes closed in prayer, soldiers and policemen surrounded us. Some of us had our arms and legs broken. Twenty-five students were killed instantly. One woman was eight months pregnant. . . She had a miscarriage there and then. Was all this reported or mentioned on the radio? The Voice of Truth? No! All that the Voice of Truth had to say was that the university was closed because the students went on strike over food. That's a lie. I was there! I am a witness! I just escaped miraculously. But I have learned something else. His Excellency Ole Excellence means business. I have stopped asking too many questions. Democracy here means, first, fending for oneself. So I'll finish my studies first, get myself a job at the bank and acquire a few things of my own. Or else I shall get myself a scholarship, go to the USA and come back and start a private research institute. I'll become a consultant for Western companies and governments. But I have a question. Where can one find something one can appropriate for oneself? If you have any more questions you'd better go to the teacher of modern stars. . ."

There are two types of modern students, Matigari thought to himself: those who love the truth, and those who sell the truth. What about the modern teachers? Teachers of modern stars? On parting, he said to the student:

"Great fear breeds great misery in the land. Give a little sacrifice to appease a thieving evil spirit, and this will only whet its appetite and greed for more. . ."

15

The teacher was in his house, pen in hand. When he saw Matigari, he felt suddenly weak. His welcome to Matigari came in the form of a question.

"What do you want?"

"I have been roaming all over —"

"So you haven't heard the news yet?" He cut him short.

"What news?"

"They are looking for you."

"Hunting for one who's hunting for the truth?"

"As the saying goes, the hunter may very well find himself hunted. This country has changed from what it was yesterday, or what it was when we fought for it. We have no part to play in it any more. I'm thinking of going to a country where there aren't as many problems as here."

"There are two worlds," Matigari said to the teacher. "There is the world of those who accept things as they are, and there is that of those who want to change things. Which world do you belong to?"

"What? Change? Revolution? Are you one of those radicals who talk about revolution? I think that it's better that you leave. I don't want your radicalism to rub off on me. Revolution is like leprosy. . ."

"You won't tell me where I can find it?"

"Find what? Leprosy?"

"Truth. And justice. When we were in prison, didn't I hear you ask: If I cannot teach the truth, what should I teach, then? Since we parted I haven't slept a wink. I haven't rested either. I have wandered all over the country looking for somebody who can tell me where a person who has girded himself with a belt of peace can find truth and justice! In the wilderness, I met a woman who said to me: Go to those who teach modern wisdom, the modern wise men of modern stars. That is why I am here. Take your chalk or your pen and tell me! Where in this country can a person girded with a belt of peace find truth and justice?"

"*Sssssshhh*, stop talking so loudly," the teacher cautioned him. "Yesterday is gone and forgotten. Today is a new day. Tomorrow will be another day. Didn't you hear that teachers and lecturers are being detained without trial? Look at me. I have a wife and two children. What will they eat if I am sent to prison? And all for asking too many questions! The "thief" told us that there is a lot of wisdom in learning to keep one's lips sealed. He ought to have added that there are people who reap benefits from singing the approved tune, those who dance in step with the approved dance. I have since been ordained into the order of cowardice and have joined the ranks of those whose lips are sealed. You'd better go. . . No, wait a minute. . . I've thought of something else. . . Listen. If you really want to find the answers to your questions you should go to the priest. He never puts down his Bible. He does nothing else but read the Bible all day long and interpret it to the people. He might be able to tell you all about truth and justice. . ."

Matigari looked at the teacher. The teacher's eyes were filled with intense fear. His face was streaming with sweat.

"Let me tell you something," Matigari said. "I have just come from seeing the student of modern stars. I told him that too much fear breeds misery in the land. . . Far better are those who are going to gaol singing songs of courage rooted in their commitment to truth and justice. . . What else did I tell him? There are two types of the wise ones of the stars: those who love the truth, and those who sell the truth."

16

He found the priest kneeling in prayer. A Bible lay open in front of him. He wore a cassock and a white dog-collar. He looked as though he were preparing to go and perform a ceremony.

Matigari stood just inside the doorway.

The priest remained absorbed in this prayer posture. He was greatly worried by the rumors that Jesus had returned. Suppose there were truth in them? He was now asking God for guidance on the matter just in case. . .

. . . *just as you said, Lord, that we should keep our lamps ready at all times like the five wise maidens. For two people will be in the fields; the one shall be taken and the other left. Two women shall be grinding the mill; the one shall be taken, and the other will be left behind. You should always be ready, for none knows when the Lord will return. . . But remember, O Lord, that you also said that, since nobody knows the time of your returning, day or night, minute or hour, we should therefore be aware of false prophets. For there will come those who come to deceive the hearts of the elect, and false Christs and false prophets will arise. That is why I am praying, Lord, that you open my eyes and my ears so that I may see and hear you, no matter how you are dressed. For you also said that when you return you will remove from your sight those who never came to see you when you were in prison or in hospital, those who did not feed you when you were hungry or give you water when you were thirsty! Such people will cry unto you, saying: When did we see you hungry or thirsty or naked or ill or in prison and did not tend to you? And you will tell them: Just as you did not for the least of those among you, so you did not unto me —* "

Matigari cleared his throat. The priest stopped abruptly and leaped to his feet. The sweat that had broken on his brow made it glisten. His heart was beating heavily, but he tried to steel himself.

"Who are you?" he asked Matigari.

Before Matigari could answer, the priest remembered his prayer and how those who had not tended to the least among them would be thrown into the everlasting fire, and he hurriedly began doing good deeds to Matigari, driven by doubt and fear!

"Please sit down!" He gave Matigari a seat and started to welcome him with kindly words. "I know I shouldn't ask, but are you hungry?"

"Not really."

"Are you feeling ill at all?"

"No."

"You are not thirsty, are you?"

"No."

"And you don't have any problems at all. . . such as lack of clothes, or shelter perhaps?"

"My thirst and hunger are not for material things. My only thirst and hunger are to do with my troubled spirit. I have travelled far and wide looking for truth and justice."

"Truth and justice?"

"Yes."

"Have you been to church?"

"No. I don't belong to your religions or to your churches. But a weary bird will perch and nest on any tree. I have searched in market-places, in shops, at crossroads, in the fields, in the courts of law and even in the wilderness. I have walked. I have ridden in *matatus,* on donkey carts, buses, lorries, trains and boats. I have been to the police, to the judges, to all the different government officers. I have been to students, to teachers, but all in vain. None of these people were able to answer my questions. Finally somebody told me. Go to the modern wise men of God. That is who you are, isn't it?"

"Yes, you have come to the right place."

"You read and interpret God's words. Let me unload on you a burden which is weighing heavily on me. I shall not keep anything away from you for sound advice can only be given in reply to frank words. Long ago, there was a young woman. She was the purest of maids. She had spent all her life obeying two masters: the heavenly Father, and her earthly father. She never failed to attend prayer-meetings and she always went to church. During the war for independence, her earthly father was arrested by the police. They told her that she could save him only by surrendering her purity. She refused, and her father was hanged. She was left to look after her brothers and sisters. So she said to her heavenly Father: Help me take care of my family. She prayed and prayed. But there was no food to eat, and there were no clothes to wear! So she decided to walk the streets. She needed money to buy food and clothes. However, from that day she swore to herself: Lord, give me the strength never to go to bed with those who killed my father, or with any of their kind. Give me the strength, sinner though I be, give me the courage, to obey this eleventh commandment! The years went by. Then a man came out of the forest, where the guerrillas fighting for the land had based themselves. He found policemen setting a dog on the young woman. They wanted favors from her. But she would not have anything to do with them. The man rescued her. Soon after that, the man was thrown into prison. The young woman went and gave herself to one of the policemen, who, after he had had his fill was gripped by that sleep which comes over us men after such events. The young woman took the keys and gave them to a boy with whom she had arranged all this. The boy went and opened up the cell, letting out the man and ten other prisoners. The boy locked up the cell and returned the keys to the young woman, who in turn put them back into the policeman's pocket, and she pretended to sleep. When the policeman woke up, he found the young woman still asleep next to him. He hurriedly got up, so that his superiors would not find him sleeping in the office. The young woman went away. But she was filled with grief. She had finally broken her eleventh commandment. . . Tell, me, you who read and interpret the words of God: Where lies truth in this matter? Where lies justice? Where are truth and justice to be found on this earth? Because I know that, wherever that young woman is, she is in tears. What have you to say? With what words would you wipe away her tears? The Father in heaven, why did He create a world that was so upside-down? A world in which those who sow evil reap good, and those who sow good reap evil! What do the holy books you study have to say about all this? Tell me the answer to the riddle. Untie this knot for me. Tell me: What shall I say to the young woman? For I told her I would not go back to see her until I had found the answers to her questions. . ."

The priest felt at peace; a heavy burden had been lifted from his soul. So the prison doors had not really opened mysteriously. So all those tales about Gabriel were mere gossip. Yet one should always keep one's lamp ready just in case. He cleared his throat and then said:

"The riddle is a difficult one to solve. But there is nothing that the Lord in heaven does without a good reason behind it. Famine, hunger, disease, pain, droughts, floods, earthquakes, death, every pestilence — they all have a purpose. God works in mysterious ways, and He reveals the purpose of his actions only when and if He wishes, or when the time is ripe. We can never rush God's decision. Pain and suffering are a test of our faith and our capacity to endure. If the girl had not forsaken the church, God would surely have shown her the way. But who am I to pass judgment over another? Who am I to stand between a person and their decision before their God? Do you remember the story of the woman who was found with a man who was not her husband? What did Jesus say to her when she was taken to him? *Let him who has no sin cast the first stone,* yes, throw the first stone. I shall now follow in the footsteps of Christ and say: Let him who has no sin cast the first stone. But I say to the girl: Come back to church and kneel down before God. Ask Him for forgiveness. . ."

Without realizing it, Matigari gave away the young woman's name.

"But what sin has Gũthera committed? Between Gũthera and God, who has really sinned against the other? Who of the two should kneel down before the other and ask for forgiveness? Tell me, you who read holy books: Who created a world so upside-down?"

"Stop there! Just stop there before you commit the sin that will never be forgiven!" the priest said quickly, shocked by Matigari's words. "What devil is this that has come to my house?" Then, on remembering what he had read in the Bible, and also the rumors in the country, he once again felt uneasy. Doubts assailed him. Might not these trials be the same as those which God put to Job when He allowed Satan to try him?"

"What sin?" Matigari asked in a voice full of pain.

"Blasphemy! The sin of abusing the Holy Spirit!"

"Just because I said this world is upside-down? Let me tell you yet another riddle concerning him-who-sows and him-who-reaps-where-he-never-sowed. He-who-sows cleared the bush, cultivated the land, flattened it, sowed and tended the crop. He-who-reaps -where-he-never-sowed grabbed the land, and it was he who took home the harvest. He-who-sows then built a house; he-who-reaps-where-he-never-sowed grabbed it. He-who-sows made goods in industries, and he-who-reaps-where-he-never-sowed came and took them. He-who-sows made some clothes, and he-who-reaps-where-he-never-sowed came and took these too. Whatever he-who-sows produced with his sweat and labor, he-who-reaps-where-he-never-sowed would help himself to it. So he-who-sows composed a song of resistance:

I will not produce food
For him-who-reaps-where-he-never-sowed to feed on it
While I go to sleep on an empty belly.
I will not build a house
For him-who-reaps-where-he-never-sowed to sleep in it
While I sleep in the open.
I will not sew clothes
For him-who-reaps-where-he-never-sowed to wear them
While I strut about naked.
I will not make goods
For him-who-reaps-where-he-never-sows to grow rich
While I remain empty-handed.
I have refused to be like the cooking pot
Whose sole purpose is to cook and never to eat!

"Wise man! War broke out between him-who-reaps-where-he-never-sowed and him-who-sowed. But he-who-reaps was not alone. He and his servants chased the sower over many hills, down through many valleys, up many mountains, in caves, ditches, plains, forests, all over the country. They fought. One year. Ten years. So many years. He-who-sows first knocked down the servant. Finally he put his foot on the chest of him-who-reaps-where-he-never-sowed. He sang victory songs and set out on his way. Home! And who do you think he found at the gate of his house? None other than the son of him-who-reaps-where-he-never-sowed, accompanied by his servant. They are the ones who called the police and got him arrested. You, wise man, did you say that this world is not upside-down? A world in which:

The builder sleeps in the open,
The worker is left empty-handed,
The tailor goes naked,
And the tiller goes to sleep on an empty stomach?

"Tell me! Where are the truth and justice in all this? Where in this world can one find justice?"

By now the priest was getting a little impatient with the man's questions and long stories. The fear that had earlier overcome him, because of the rumors of Christ's Second Coming, was now all but gone. There was no way Jesus would have come back to ask such foolish questions and to tell political fables. He yawned. Then, looking at his watch, he said:

"You know, the sun never stops to let the king go by. I have a ceremony to perform elsewhere. You've asked me two questions, and I will endeavor to answer them.

"It is true that this world is upside-down. That is precisely why God sent His only son to come here and set it to rights with His eternal love. Go tell Gũthera — isn't that what you called the woman? Tell her this: When people grieve over their sins they must know that they will never find peace unless they go to the Cross! When a sinner leaves his sins behind, and returns to the Lord, he is good and is full of forgiveness. You should worry less about the sins you committed before you knew the Lord, but more about those you have committed from the moment you realized that you are a sinner. Christ is the only one who can right a world which is upside-down. He is the only one who can set right souls which have gone astray. . .

"On matters of politics — like the question of finding the truth and justice on earth — I will answer you the way Jesus answered the Pharisees who had gone to test him and confuse him with questions about earthly rule although they knew very well that his kingdom was in heaven whose capital city was the New Jerusalem. Jesus told them: Render unto Caesar what is Caesar's, and unto God what is God's. So today I also say to you: If you want to know of heavenly truth and justice, you should turn to the Lord God of heaven, who is the same Jesus Christ who was once crucified on the Cross for the sake of you and me. But as far as earthly truth and justice are concerned, you should go to those who rule here on earth. . .

"I'll give you some advice, though. We are very lucky in this country because his Excellency Ole Excellence loves and believes in Christianity. He is also a very enlightened man. He has a ministry which deals with the issues of truth and justice. The Minister for Truth and Justice (he too, like the President, never misses a church service) is coming to pay a visit to the residents of this area. As you know, he often tours various places, telling people how best to abide peaceably by the law. For example, he will address the people this evening at the council's social hall, with regard to the never-ending strikes that take place at the factory here. Please go to the Minister for Truth and Justice and ask him: Where can one find truth and justice on this earth?"

17

The meeting called by the Minister for Truth and Justice was well attended, because people had been told that he was going to resolve the dispute between the workers and the factory owners. The Provincial Commissioner had also toured a number of villages in the region, telling people about the minister's visit. A lot of dignitaries were present. There were representatives from ministries from the ruling party, from the county councils, from the churches and from the factory. The workers and their sympathizers were there *en masse.*

The country had a good international image in the West because of its rule of 'truth and justice'. The meeting had therefore drawn observers from the ruling political parties of the Western countries. They sat in the front-row seats, so that they could properly see how the workers in a Third World country could be silenced with instant truth and justice!

The riot-control police and a unit of the army were present, and they stood in battle formation outside the social hall. Inside the hall were more armed policemen. They stood leaning against the wall, their eyes fixed on the crowd.

The minister wore a dark suit with gray stripes. The party tie of red and green stripes was tucked well inside his waistcoat so that only the top part of it was visible. The tie had the emblem of the ruling party — a picture of a parrot — and the letters KKK, the initials of the party. A red carnation hung from the lapel of the jacket, and a white handkerchief peeped out of the breast pocket. John Boy and Robert Williams sat on his right-hand side, and the church minister, the Provincial Commissioner and the Member of Parliament for the area sat on his left. District commissioners and district officers sat on either side of these guests. In the rows immediately behind the minister there sat some white, brown and black men, dressed in judicial robes. Next to them were three others. One was the editor of the newspaper the *Daily Parrot.* Another was Professor of the History of Parrotology, and the third a university lecturer who had a B.Ed., an MA and a Ph.D. in the philosophy of Parrotology. The three held a hymn-book, *Songs of a Parrot* which had been composed by a group of specialists in the voices of parrots.

Behind them all stood the Commissioner of Police. At one corner there sat a hooded informer, completely covered in a cone-shaped white cloth with only three slits: for the eyes, and for his mouth.

The same dull atmosphere which had prevailed in the country the whole day also filled the hall. It was neither hot nor cold. The murmuring of those assembled indicated neither happiness nor sadness. The electric light was weak, giving a kind of twilight. Nothing was clear.

Everyone waited.

The priest opened the meeting with a prayer: "Our Lord in heaven, give guidance to your servant, the Minister for Truth and Justice, so that he can correctly interpret your will. O Lord, still the hearts of the employers, and those of the workers, so that they may all be satisfied with the decisions arrived at through truth and justice."

After the prayer, the Provincial Commissioner introduced the minister to "your subjects." The minister then stood up and began his speech.

"I shall not beat about the bush. I shall speak the plain truth and in justice. I am the soul of this government. I am the soul of this nation. I am the light in the dark tunnel. I am the torch of development. Why do I say this? Because, without the rule of law — truth and justice — there is no government, no nation, no civilization. The rule of law is the true measure of *civilization*. I should know. I was brought up in the law. I abide by the law, and the law abides in me. I have been taught the law, and I staunchly believe in it. I am the guardian of the law today. I make the law, and I ensure that it is kept. My father was the first person in this country to advocate loyalism to the Crown at the beginning of the century. Some might wonder: Loyalty to whose law? The colonial law? Let me tell you: Law is law. Those who realized this from the beginning are the only people of any worth in this country today. Yes, we loyalists are the ones in power today. Long live loyalism! Let me explain. Look at John Boy here. He and I went to school together. Isn't that so Johnny Boy? We first went to Fort Hare in South Africa. We were also in Britain together. Do you remember our digs in Islington? We nicknamed you, "Bookworm" because you were always cramming. Do you remember? He-he-he!"

"But you know your friends were sons of Kabakas and Cerere

Khamas — sons of chiefs and kings," John Boy now answered, grinning from ear to ear. "We nicknamed you "Style," "Mr. Style" because you did everything *in style.* Do you remember that funny little Goan lawyer who used to silence everyone with arguments about Lenin, Trotsky and Stalin? Do you remember how you once silenced him when you told him —"

"I am an African Anglophile and proud of it!" the minister and John Boy said in chorus as though performing some theatrical act on stage. They both laughed.

"Yes, this Boy you see here — his father was killed by terrorists for obeying and abiding by the law. Look at how far his son has gone today. Is he scavenging for rubbish in garbage yards? You'd all agree with me that it is clear that he is not! Look at me. I have a seven-storied house here. I have three swimming-pools. . . yes, three. . . one for the children, one for the guests and one for me and my wife! I have also got saunas modeled on those in Finland! The house is decorated with marble, from Italy. *Imported Italian marble!* I have what the English lords call a *family coat of arms,* in other words, the emblem of the house. My coat of arms is a picture of a coffee bush, guarded over by two whips. Below this is *the family motto:* Destroy Terrorists. Look at anybody who is worth anything, be he from this tribe or that; they are all those who have been abiding by the law ever since the colonial times. What about the children of those who took axes and home-made guns, claiming that they were going to fight against the rule of law? Where are they today? Where is the independence that we fought for? That is what they are still shouting at the bottom of the ladder.

"In fact, it is we who abided by the law who prevented the country from being destroyed. If you look at the situation dispassionately, without the kind of *distortion* you find with some of those *fiction* writers, you can see that it is those who obeyed the colonial law who brought about independence. Wasn't it only the other day that all the university professors and specialists in Parrotology had a history conference? What do they teach us? That, according to their research, those who joined hands with colonialists in protecting the law — *loyalists* — are really the ones who made the colonialists give us independence on a platter. I have ordered all those loyalist professors and all holders of Ph.D.s in Parrotology to be promoted and given permanent professorships.

For these professors are different from those who are always rais-
ing a hue and cry about revolution, revolutionary politics, revolutionary socialism and other *foreign ideologies*. No! These
permanent professors are the ones who know how to obey and
abide by the law, how to serve the law. You agree with me,
Professor, don't you?"

The Permanent Professor in the History of Parrotology shot
up at once. So did the Ph.D. in Parrotology and the Editor of the
Daily Parrot. They sang three stanzas from *Songs of a Parrot* and
then sat down, clinging to the hymn-book as though their lives
depended on it.

The minister was very pleased with the rendering of the song,
saying that, if they continued in that way, they might be on the
following year's honors list and that they would receive decora-
tions such as GKM (The President's Ears) or MMT (Eyes of the
State).

"I hope that you have heard the truth for yourselves," he continued. "If it were not for us loyalists, what independence would
you be enjoying today? Tell me, what independence? Of the grave-
yards? You should count yourselves lucky that the government is
led by a man who is merciful and a Christian. Just imagine, the
other day some people at the barracks took to arms in order to
mutiny. Army mutiny! Did they want a *coup* or what? They won't
even give us a chance to ensure that the fires of independence
continue burning steadily! Why did they not mutiny during the
colonial rule? And these students here demonstrating outside
Western embassies simply because these governments are helping *South Africa!* Why can't these students follow the footsteps of
the permanent professors in Parrotology? How can we dictate to
other countries what they should do with their own money? Even
His Excellency Ole Excellence has gone a bit too far with his
beliefs in this democracy! Imagine if this were one of those countries which does not believe in the rule of law; or imagine what
would have happened if the government of this country had fall-
en into the hands of those who had taken up axes to fight the
law? Yes. . . if the government had been taken by terrorists. . . In
other words, *if this were a gangster government,* what do you think
would have happened to those university students?

"Listen! Let me drop another hint. The government knows that
those subversive elements were not alone. The brains behind these

people's actions have discovered another way of bringing confusion in the country. *Uvumi*- rumor-mongering. There is now a terrible rumor going round these villages that Christ has come back. I have just one question that I would like to put to you: How can Jesus Christ return without first revealing himself to his disciples? Here on this platform we have a church minister. Minister, please tell everyone here now whether or not Jesus has come back. Has Jesus Christ come back?"

The priest stood up, clinging to his Bible. He first looked around him, for he still was not so sure about the rumors before addressing the crowd with the following words.

"I shall read a passage from the gospel according to the Book of Matthew, chapter 24, verse 23: Then if any man shall say unto you, Lo, here is Christ, or there, believe it not. For there shall arise false Christs, and false prophets, and shall show great signs and wonders insomuch that if it were possible, they shall deceive the very elect. Behold, I have told you before."

The priest sat down. The minister continued:

"You have now heard the word of God for yourselves! That you should ignore false prophets, false angels and false Christs.

"Let me come to another point. The *uvumi* we have been warned against by the priest was started last night by a group of thieves and murderers — a group of criminals, in other words— who escaped from prison yesterday. They are the ones who started and spread the rumor that it was Gabriel the Angel of God who had opened the prison doors. I shall tell you the truth. The ea:s of the government, and the eyes of the government are everywhere: in police and prison cells, in shopping centers, in workplaces, in schools, in churches, in market-places and even in the walls and the very foundations of your houses. Our hands are longer than the longest road, and they travel faster than the speed of lightning. All those who escaped are in the hands of the government."

When he got to the end of the sentence, two policemen ushered the peasant, the "thief", the "murderer", the "vagrant", the student, the "pickpocket", the worker, the teacher and the drunkard into the hall. The only two people missing from the group were Gĩcerũ* and Matigari.

---

*Gĩcerũ: a proper name, here also meaning the "informer".

"You have now seen them for yourselves, haven't you?" the minister said pointing at the prisoners. "Yes, these are the people who last night escaped from prison and started spreading rumors that it was the Angel Gabriel who had let them out. They did not realize that one of the government's own eyes was among them. They did not realize that with them was the government's ear. The government knows exactly who those Gabriels are: the teacher and the student. Imagine, these two were teaching Marxism even in prison. This Karl Marx has really made these students and teachers crazy. But they are cowards really. These two had locked themselves away reading Karl Marx. Take them all away! Their cases will be heard and settled just now. . . The Permanent Professor of the History of Parrotology, the Ph.D.. in Parrotology and the Editor of the *Daily Parrot will* give evidence to show that, historically, philosophically and journalistically speaking, it is those who teach Marxism — in other words, communism — who spoil our students and our workers. That is why they should be detained without trial. Isn't that so, Professor?"

The permanent professor, the Ph.D. holder and the newspaper editor stood up and sang three verses from *Songs of a Parrot*. After they had finished they sat down, still holding the song-book very tightly.

The minister then said to the police:

"Do your work."

The policeman pushed the prisoners into a room at the back of the hall.

"The only person we haven't caught up with is the one calling himself Matigari ma Njirũũngi. But he too should be warned. The hand of the law is longer than any road he may decide to walk on. Let me now put a stop to all this *uvumi* in the country, especially in the villages around here. There are no freedom fighters in the forests. They all came out of the forest at independence when the flag was hoisted. All those who refused to come out were shot down. *Full stop.* Let him who has ears listen. And he who has not got any should borrow his mother's.

"Let me now come to the purpose of my visit here: the dispute between the workers and the owners of the leather and plastic factory. But before I go any further, I am told that there is to be a small ceremony. . ."

Robert Williams and John Boy Junior stood up immediately. Robert Williams handed a check and certificates to John Boy. John Boy in his turn handed them over to the minister. They both sat down.

The minister looked at the check and the certificates, smiled, held them in one hand and then continued with his speech, obviously invigorated by what he had received from Boy and Williams.

"Let me first thank the directors of this company for the work that they have done. Do you see this cheque? Look at it carefully. We like doing things in the open. Christian democracy. Honesty. This is a cheque for 50,000 shillings towards the special presidential fund for handicapped children. This company is truly one with a human heart and a human face! Thank you. Aren't you going to clap? Give warm applause! Again! That's it! Do you see these certificates? These are for *personal shares*. They are for His Excellency Ole Excellence. The other one here is for me, again *personal shares*. Just stop whistling for a while. You will be able to do that much better after you've heard everything. Donating *personal shares* is nothing really special. A lot of companies have already done that. But the most impressive thing this company has done, *a real revolutionary step,* is that they have given the ruling party a few shares. Do you know the significance of that?

"The ruling party is our party. It is your party. It is the national party. Therefore this company has given shares to the country, the whole nation. From now onwards, all of you here and even those who are not here have a stake in the company. Now this company is yours. It is ours. It is a national company. This is *capitalism with a socialist face* - or *socialism with a capitalist heart*. That is to say *true African socialism*. Not like that of Karl Marx and Lenin that the students and teachers are always talking about. *Lakini watona cha mtema kuni!**

"They will have to take those revolutions of theirs back to the Soviet Union, China, North Korea, Cuba or Albania. Why can't they learn and teach the kind of socialism we have been shown by the leather and plastics factory? Why are you not applauding? Why aren't you women ululating over what the company has done? Well, it takes a bit of time for the real significance of certain things to sink in, I know it will in due course; so it does not matter!"

**Lakini watona cha mtema kuni* (Kiswahili): "they will be dealt with."

The permanent professor, the Ph.D. and the newspaper editor made as if they were about to stand and sing a few more stanzas from *Songs of a Parrot*. But the minister, embarrassed by their readiness to sing, asked them to wait for a little while.

"Now, even if you were the one arbitrating between the company and the factory workers, you would see that the dispute has now been resolved more or less. From now onwards, anyone who goes on strike against this company will actually be striking against the government. Provoking this company will be exactly the same as sticking a finger in the nose of the ruling party. Hurling abuse at this company is the same as hurling insults at the nation.

'I shall now give the verdict on the dispute between the employers and the workers. Firstly, I want all the workers to go back to work now and end the strike immediately. Is that clear? From this minute on, the strike is over. And I order the company to take back all the workers, with the exception of the ringleaders. Why do I order the company to do so? Because the company has already decided to sack all those who went on strike and employ those who spend their time queuing for work instead. I think that such a solution to the dispute is a good and just one. Who is that booing?

"Before I finish, I would like to remind the masses wherever they are that strikes are banned by a presidential decree. Before, in colonial times, we used to go on strike demanding our independence. But what other independence are we striking for? This is your government! This is a workers' government! Furthermore, His Excellency Ole Excellence is a worker, a first-class worker. Number one. So this government is led by a worker. What more do you want? Are there any questions?"

Ngarūro wa Kīrīro stood up:

"Speaking on behalf of the workers, I would like to say that a dispute or disagreement is always between two parties. Our dispute is between the company owners and the workers. Ours is a dispute between labor and capital. But the owners of capital should always remember that even the capital in question comes from the labor of our hands. Your verdict only shows that you — the government and the ruling party — are on the side of capital, on the side of those who own companies and large farms. I have only one question: Where is our government, we workers? We are not asking for other people's property. We are only asking for adequate remuneration for our labor. The labor of our hands is all we own. It is our only property. We sell this labor in the labor market. Tell me, you who go to the market-places: If the buyer refuses to pay the price being asked for by the seller, has the latter not got the right to refuse to part with the wares until he gets a suitable price for them? Or one agreed upon between the buyer and the seller? Our strike action is just such a refusal. We are withdrawing our labor from the market until the buyer agrees to meet our price. We cannot go back to work unless our demands are met. All we are asking for are wage increases to meet the ever-spiraling prices of goods. We are also asking that the wages be increased in proportion to the rate of inflation. We also ask for Saturdays off, or to be paid *overtime* for working on Saturdays. We also demand that John Boy Junior and Robert Williams be removed from the board of directors, and to have new directors appointed in their place. The two are worse than those who were there during the colonial days."

Ngarũro wa Kĩrĩro sat down. The workers applauded, with the women ululating.

The minister waited for the applause to die down. Then he said, "You have heard the insolence for yourselves, haven't you? That man has just broken the law three times over. Firstly, he has defied my order; and secondly he, has defied two presidential decrees. He has defied the order which I announced here a few minutes ago, in everyone's hearing. I just announced the end of the strike, didn't I? It ended the moment I finished speaking. Therefore this man is actually asking people to go on strike again. In doing so, he is urging people to defy the special decree by the President. Do you know which law he is breaking by asking people to disobey His Excellency? The law of *sedition* and *treason*. And now it is my turn to ask a question: How can industries run if the workers are the ones who are to decide who is to be employed and what wages are to be paid? And how can the industries run if it is the workers who decide when they want to work and when they want to rest? If they feel so strongly about these things, why don't they employ themselves, instead of going to seek employment in other people's firms? The man who has just spoken has refused to work. Everyone here is a witness to that. It is his right to opt out of work, but he should not incite others to follow his example. How can such a person who clearly chooses not to work be helped? Police! Do your duty! Maybe he is one of those who are preaching the teachings of Karl Marx in the country."

Two policemen grabbed Ngarūro wa Kīrīro, and they threw him into the room where the other prisoners were. People started shouting and arguing. The police commissioner blew his whistle. The riot police stood in the doorway and at the windows. A hush fell over the room. The people were trapped inside the room.

"Are there any more questions?"

His voice was greeted by a deep silence. He continued speaking as though nothing much had happened.

"Are there any other questions?"

This too met a deep silence. The Minister for Truth and Justice continued, "Why don't you want to ask questions? You do realize that we have some guests from Western countries here — USA, Britain, West Germany, France — and they are running a course on behalf of the ruling party on Party Organization and Responsible Trade Unionism, here in this country. I want them to see *African socialism* at work. Here, in this country, we are guided by democracy and the rule of law. The only thing we never condone is the breaking of the law. So the government has the democratic right to remove such a person from amidst the people. No government can allow 0.0001 per cent of the people to disrupt the rights of the other 99.9999 per cent. How can one rotten grain of corn be allowed to make a whole sack go to waste? *Even the majority have human rights too!*

"Is there another question?"

"Yes!" a voice said.

Everyone turned their eyes to the door. A tall, well-built, elderly man stood in the doorway. On his head was a wide-brimmed hat, strapped under his chin. Around it was a strap decorated with beads, and an ostrich feather. He wore a kneelength coat, made of leopard skin. He wore corduroy trousers. His hands were inside his coat pockets, as though he were holding something.

Gūthera and Mūriūki exchanged glances.

Everyone stood in silent anticipation. They could not believe that anybody could be so brave as to ask a question after what had happened to Ngarūro wa Kīrīro, and now that they were all trapped inside the hall by armed police and soldiers.

Matigari and the Minister for Truth and Justice stood facing each other.

Two policemen made as if to arrest Matigari. Keeping his eyes fixed on the minister, Matigari spoke in such a way that everyone in the room could hear his words clearly. With a firm voice he warned the two policemen, "Don't you dare touch me! I am as old as this country." There was not the slightest trace of fear in his voice. The courage and the strength in his voice made the policemen start. John Boy Junior and Robert Williams whispered something to each other, but they kept their eyes on Matigari all the time. The police chief went and murmured to the minister, while keeping his eyes fixed on Matigari's hands, which were still inside the coat, "He might have a gun. Make him keep on talking until we find a way of shooting him."

The minister found his tongue. "Leave him alone," he said, in a voice that was louder than necessary. "I said that whoever wished to ask a question may do so. This is a free country, not like Russia or China."

Matigari moved into the middle of the crowd. As he began to speak, still holding his hands in his pockets, none dared to cough or make the slightest noise.

"You have asked why nobody wants to ask questions. I will answer you. Taking precaution does not mean that one is a coward. Leopard once asked hare: My friend, why don't you ever pay me a visit? Hare answered: I have seen a lot of people enter your house, but I have never seen even one of them leaving. All the people you see here are like hare. They have eyes and ears to see and hear whatever is happening around them. But still, I will tell them this: Too much fear breeds misery in the land. So knowing full well what hare told leopard, I will put a question to the Minister for Truth and Justice. For I have spent the whole day roving around the whole country, looking for somebody who could give me an answer to my question. Yes, I have walked and have traveled by *matatus* and by all sorts of vehicles. I have spoken to medicine men, students, teachers and the wise men of modern stars. One wise man, reader of God's words, told me: Go to the Minister for Truth and Justice. I obeyed the priest.

This is my question:

The builder builds a house.
The one who watched while it was being built moves into it.
The builder sleeps in the open air,
No roof over his head.

The tailor makes clothes.
The one who does not even know how to thread a needle wears
   the clothes.
The tailor walks in rags.

The tiller tends crops in the fields.
The one who reaps-where-he-never-sowed yawns for having
   eaten too much.
The tiller yawns for not having eaten at all.

The worker produces goods.
Foreigners and parasites dispose of them.
The worker is left empty handed.

Where are truth and justice on this earth?"

The Minister for Truth and Justice paused for a while and
struck a contemplative mood before answering.

"Stop speaking in parables. If you want to ask a question, then
do so in plain language. You have nothing to fear. So now, pour
out all your problems and you will soon see. The preacher did
the right thing to send you to me. Yes, he did the right thing."

"Mine is not a long story," Matigari said, "but it is not a short
one either. It is the story you now see in this very room. My story
is made up of you and me. I built a house. I cultivated the land.
I worked the industry. But Settler Williams, aided by his servant,
John Boy, ended up with all the wealth. I said to myself: The differences between the robber and the robbed can only be settled
in struggle. So out in the fields we went, Williams and his servant
Boy on one side, and I on the other. For many seasons we hunted one another. We went over many mountains, through many
years. We hunted each other, trying to see who would be the first
to bring down the other. I first tried to bring down Boy. The settler was nothing without the support of his servant. Settler Williams
could never rock the foundations of my home without a collabo-
rator. I finally managed to bring both of them down. Boy fell first;
then Settler Williams. Yesterday I returned home. My heart was
full of joy, and my whole being was ringing with victory. But who
do I find standing at the gate of my house? Boy's son, together
with Settler William's son. They asked me: Where is the title-deed
to this house? I in turn asked them: What title-deed other than my

sweat, my blood? They refused to return the keys to my house, but instead they called the police. I was thrown into gaol. Over there are Boy's son the settler's son and the police commissioner. Ask them if what I am saying is not true. All I demand in this land of democracy is truth and justice."

Robert Williams and John Boy were still whispering to each other. Boy scribbled a note, which he handed to the police chief.

"Who are you?" the minister asked.

"Matigari ma Njirũũngi," he answered.

The minister started. He took out a handkerchief from his pocket and wiped his face. The police chief whispered to the minister again. They all still thought that Matigari had a gun in his pocket. Why else did he keep his hands in his pockets? And indeed, how come he was so daring? But there was no way they could have shot Matigari without endangering the other people, and particularly the very important guests, who were seated on the platform. Matigari stood in the midst of the people. And the people stood silently with total admiration. What a long time it had been since they had last seen such courage! So it was true that the patriots of long ago were still alive! So the patriots of the land had finally returned to help them claim their own! The police chief watched Matigari carefully. His eyes remained fixed on Matigari's hands. Slowly ever so slowly, he lowered his own to his hip. He surreptitiously began to unfasten the holster.

The minister said, "Oh. . . Matigari ma Njirũũngi! Come forward! Let us have a good look at you."

The policemen started making a move towards Matigari. But Matigari said, "Don't touch me! I can take myself."

People made way for him. As for the guests on the platform, they all had the same thoughts in their minds. Their eyes converged at Matigari's hands. The priest's lips moved rapidly in silent prayer.

As Matigari drew closer to the platform, the police chief suddenly whipped a pistol from the holster and pointed it at Matigari, shouting, "Hands up!"

Matigari took his hands out of his pockets, grinning as he suddenly realized how frightened the police chief was and why. Then he said, "I have girded myself with a belt of peace."

But the police chief was not satisfied. He waved at two policemen and indicated to them to search Matigari.

He had no gun, no knife, not even the least of weapons. Yet still they handcuffed him. It was no good taking chances with such a character.

All the guests on the platform took their handkerchiefs out of their pockets at about the same time. They felt relieved. Matigari was taken into the little room, where Ngarūro wa Kīrīro and the others were. The only person who was not in the group of those who had escaped from prison now was Gīcerū.

The police chief put back the pistol into its holster, looking a little embarrassed for having betrayed so much fear in front of all those people.

The minister appeared uneasy. He was confused as to where to pick up the threads from. He coughed as if to clear his throat:

"Even those who like to blame the government for everything can now see for themselves! What would they suggest that the government did with such a person? You have all heard what he said! A man is arrested for trespassing on other people's property. He breaks away from prison; he roams the whole country and boasts about his exploits and his lies. To make matters worse, he has the audacity to come here in front of all these people to boast of his dastardly deeds. Yes, a criminal, a murderer and with no shame or guilt, he comes here to boast about it all.

"What sort of world would this be if those who sow are the only ones allowed to eat? Yes, what sort of world would this be if every time workers have a dispute with their employers they simply resort to arms instead of going through the proper peaceful channels so that the conflict can be settled in justice the way I have just demonstrated today? Anarchy! Yes, anarchy! Remember that a country's, any country's, welfare and stability are dependent on three kinds of people: the wealthy, like these capitalists; the soldiers, like our security forces (you all saw how swiftly the police commissioner drew his pistol); and thirdly, leaders, that is people like me, or the priest, or the others whom I shall soon introduce to you. The wealthy, the soldier, the leader — that's all we need.

"Let me show you what good leadership really means. I want all of you to see and know that I am truly the Minister for Truth and Justice. Do you see this suit that I am wearing? You see that I have an inner coat and an outer one. Why do I say this? Because it is a symbol of the two portfolios that I carry. One is for ensuring that the law is obeyed, and the other is for ensuring truth and justice. Did you see how quickly the police commissioner drew his pistol? I will now introduce to you those who bear the onerous task of meting out instant truth and justice. Do you see these gentlemen dressed in robes? They are judges and lawyers.

"I agree with the English expression *that justice delayed is justice denied.* Justice must not only be done, but must be seen to be done. So I want you to see instant justice at work. I think that I am the only minister in the whole world who travels with a whole law court, so as to be able to carry out instant justice. These gentlemen will go into that little room and hear the cases of all those who have been arrested. I shall let you know their verdict before the end of this meeting.

"These gentlemen will be assisted by the Permanent Professor of the History of Parrotology, the Editor of the *Daily Parrot*, the Ph.D. in Parrotology and the hooded informer. Do you know who the hooded justice is? He is the one wearing a white hood here. I know that in the bad colonial days you used to call him The Hood. But now we call him the Hooded Truth and Justice. He is what one might call the government's general witness whose profession is telling the truth. A professional truth-teller, if you like. These gentlemen you see here will be asking him whether the person being questioned is telling the truth or not. If he shakes his head this way or that, they will know exactly what he means. Do you know why he always tells the truth? Because he does a lot of secret investigation. . . What did I tell you? The government has eyes and ears all over. . . OK. Let's now wait for the verdict. . ."

The judges and lawyers, the permanent professor, the Ph.D. in Parrotology, the Editor of the *Daily Parrot* and the hooded justice stood up and went into the room where Matigari, Ngarũro wa Kĩrĩro and the others had been put.

"While these gentlemen are listening to the cases, I shall ask your Provincial Commissioner and the chairman of the local branch of the ruling party to say a word or two."

The Provincial Commissioner stood up. He wore khaki trousers and a matching jacket. He also wore a topi and wide-rimmed spectacles. He too wore a KKK tie. His colonial uniform seemed to weigh heavily on him. He cleared his throat in a pretentious way before beginning:

"I don't have much to say, as the minister has said everything — all that there is to be said. His decision is just and true. It is now law. If everyone abides by this new law, there will be no more conflicts. There will be abundant peace in the land. There will be no more conflict between employer and employee. . . But there are some people singing a song that could easily ruin the newly decreed peace. A little bird whispered that the song was composed by the dwellers of Trampville. The song claims that when Matigari ma Njirūūngi stamps his feet, the bullets tinkle. Tell me, you have all seen the famous Matigari whom so many have been singing about. Where are those bullets? Why did he not try to save himself with them? Matigari ma Njirūūngi is in a deep sleep — like *Rip Van Winkle*. Rip Van Winkle was a little old American who slept for a century, and by the time he woke up, he found that everything in the country had changed. Things were no longer the way he had known them to be.

"Now listen to me carefully. I have banned that song from now onwards. No song, no story or play or riddle or proverbs, mentioning Matigari ma Njirūūngi will be tolerated. All we are interested in here is *development*. We are not interested in fiction. Let us now forget that such people as Matigari ma Njirūūngi ever existed. Let us with one accord, like loyal parrots, agree that Matigari ma Njirūūngi was just a bad dream. That bit of history was just a bad dream, a nightmare in fact. We have qualified professors here who can write a new history for us.

"The village that composed the song must also change its name. How can a village call itself Trampville? Are there really any tramps living there? Are they claiming that they have nowhere to go? They should turn to the ruling party, to his Excellency Ole Excellence. They should look forward like everyone else. From now on, this village will have a new name: Progressville. And now, my good people of Progressville, forget Matigari ma Njirūūngi. Amen."

The Provincial Commissioner sat down, and the chairman of the local branch of the ruling party, Kīama Kīrīa Kīrathana (KKK), stood up.* On his shirt were a huge photograph of His Excellency and the party symbol of a parrot. Below this were the letters KKK. These initials were also on his handkerchief.

"As the chairman of the local branch of KKK. I would like to thank this *Anglo-American* company for giving *shares* to KKK. This factory now belongs to all of us. Three cheers for the com-

---

Kīama Kīrīa Kīrathana: Gīkūyū for "The Ruling Party."

pany! Down with Matigari ma Njirũũngi! Down with songs from the history of our nightmare! Now let me come to Karl Marx, the students and the workers. This Karl Marx is driving our students, lecturers and workers crazy. He should have his work permit withdrawn. I say that Karl Marx, Lenin and Mao should have no work permits in this country!"

He sang two stanzas and a chorus from *Songs of a Parrot.* He sat down.

The Member of Parliament now stood up. He wore a silk suit, a KKK tie and thick-rimmed sun-glasses. He greeted the people by singing one or two verses from *Songs of a Parrot.* Then he began to speak.

"I staunchly support all that which has already been said. But I shall add one point. It's about this Matigari ma Njirũũngi. I have been told that women around here have been singing that they will give birth to more Matigari ma Njirũũngi. Are you drunk with this Matigari ma Njirũũngi? The KKK government has said that the main cause of poverty is the fact that women breed like rats. Even during the colonial days when I worked for the *community and social welfare* department, they taught us that having too many children was dangerous. People should have children according to the size of their pockets. Those who have no money shouldn't bother to have any children. I shall get the USA to establish one of those open air birth-control clinics where women can have their wombs closed. No more children for the poor! Let us give that responsibility to the wealthy! You see, if people did not have so many children, then we would never have pay disputes, because the pay you get would suffice each worker and his wife. . . But there is an even better and more efficient method of curbing population growth. Pregnancies are the result of evil and wild desires. I shall ask the government to ban dreams and desires of that kind for a period of about two years. Fucking among the poor should be stopped by a presidential decree!"

He sat down!

The minister now spoke again.

"The villages around here are very lucky to have such leaders. I shall now call upon the preacher to read us the Ten Commandments. I want you all to listen very attentively to God's commandments."

He sat down. The priest stood up and opened his Bible. He read:

Thou shall have no other gods before me.
Thou shall not make unto thee any graven image.
Thou shall not take the name of the Lord thy God in vain.
Remember the Sabbath day, to keep it holy. Six days thou shalt
    labor; but the seventh day is the sabbath of the Lord thy God.
    In it, thou shalt not do any work.
Honor thy father and thy mother that thy days may be long upon
    the land which the Lord giveth thee.
Thou shall not kill.
Thou shall not commit adultery.
Thou shall not steal.
Thou shall not bear false witness against thy neighbor.
Thou shall not covet thy neighbor's things; thou shall not covet
    thy neighbor's wife, nor his land nor his cows nor anything
    that is thy neighbor's.

He sat down just as the judges of the court of instant truth and justice were walking back into the room, followed by the permanent professor and the hooded justice. Their leader was an old white man, who handed over the verdict to the minister.

The minister ordered that the prisoners be brought on to the platform to hear the verdict in front of everybody. The police brought them and arranged them into three groups.

"I want you, together with our visitors from USA, Britain, West Germany and France, to witness how the law works in a country under Christian democracy. In some countries I know of, criminals such as these would have been hanged, or made to face the firing-squad. But here everything must be done under the law. For instance, I am the Minister for Truth and Justice, but even I must abide by the law. So I must accept the verdict that has been reached by these gentlemen, because I too am under the law, *and I believe in the independence of the judiciary*. Right, I want you all to listen to this verdict very carefully.

"The teacher and the student will be detained without trial. The court cannot allow educated people to mislead the public with Marxist doctrines and communistic teachings."

The student and teacher were handcuffed together. In adversity, the student suddenly felt an upsurge of courage coupled with a lot of bitterness such as he had never felt before. He shouted:

"You should heed the riddle told by Matigari. A thieving spirit cannot be appeased by sacrifice. I can see that now even more
clearly. I shall sing with those who were detained yesterday, those
gaoled the day before yesterday and the fifty who were killed this
very morning by the security forces:

> Even if you detain us,
> Victory belongs to the people.
> Victory belongs to the people!"

Everybody went silent. So the rumor that fifty university students had been killed was true? A policeman covered the mouth
of the student. The teacher took over the defiance:

"I also know now that there are two truths. One truth belongs
to the oppressor; the other belongs to the oppressed! I shall never
sing like a parrot, never! I shall sing the same song of courage and
hope that was sung by the brave and courageous students."

But as he made to sing, his mouth too was covered. The student and the teacher were both taken away by prison wardens,
still resisting. *This was not justice!* From somewhere in the crowd,
a song broke out:

> Even if you kill us,
> Victory belongs to the people.
> Victory belongs to the people!

The people took up the song and sang in one voice. The
policemen cocked their guns. The Permanent Professor of the
History of Parrotology whispered something to the minister. He
in turn shouted:

"Silence! All of you, silence! I have just been told that there
are students among the people. I wish to remind them that this
village is under the control of the chief. If you want to sing, you
should sing from the official hymn-book, *Songs of a Parrot*. I don't
want to hear any more subversive songs. What you have heard
from the student is a heap of lies. The university was closed
because the students went on strike over food. . . Only one student died, trampled to death by the others. . . But we didn't come
here to talk about students. . . I shall now read the verdict that
has been arrived at by the professional judges. I want you completely to forget about the students. Right? Those who broke away

from prison are to be returned to remand prison until the day the
court gets a chance to listen to their case. They will be held in a
maximum-security prison until that time."

The police took them away. The "vagrant" caused laughter by
shouting that, since he was sure to find food and shelter in prison,
he was grateful to the judges.

"Now let us come to the case of Ngarūro wa Kīrīro. The court
is very concerned about this man. Since independence, no one
has ever stood up in public to oppose a presidential decree.
People like these sow the seeds of discord in this country. They
are the ones who are making the soldiers *mutiny*. The question
he asked shows that he is mentally deranged. The court has decided that he should be taken into a mental hospital to have his head
examined. . . So, you see, you workers were being led by a mentally deranged person."

Before he was taken away, Ngarūro wa Kīrīro shouted:

"You may arrest me, but the workers will never stop demanding back their rights!"

The minister said, "You see how the man's mind deceives
him!"

The minister now turned to Matigari ma Njirūūngi. Matigari
stood tall, fearless, full of confidence. It was this quality about him
that made people fear him. His glance was piercing, and he made
one feel as if he were looking into the very depth of one's soul.
The minister, for instance, could not look straight at Matigari's eyes.
He hesitated, seeming to have lost his tongue.

Matigari seized the opportunity, and now it looked as if it was
the minister who was on trial.

"Mr. Minister," Matigari began. "I asked you a question, but
you never answered me. I shall repeat my question. Where in this
country can a person who is girded with a belt of peace find truth
and justice?"

The minister stammered. He seemed unprepared for a repeat
of Matigari's question. He turned to the people.

"This man who calls himself Matigari ma Njirūūngi should be
hanged. Didn't you hear him confess that he was a murderer? But
the judges have found him insane. The hooded justice testified
how Matigari ma Njirūūngi shared his bread and beer in gaol in
clear imitation of Christ's Last Supper. And here you heard him
ramble on about his years in the forest and mountains, fighting

Boy and Williams. All this goes to show that such a person must be out of his mind. Major Howard Williams and John Boy went to fight against terrorists during the war for independence - well, let's call it that for lack of a better phrase. It is believed that they died fighting. They were awarded medals *in absentia* for their courage and selflessness: Williams the CBE (Commander of the British Empire), and Boy the MBE (Member of the Order of the British Empire). But if you give it a thought, do you really think that anyone in their right mind would come here to boast about how he was a murderer? And the sort of questions he is asking, are they the sort of questions which would come from sane heads like yours or mine? The court has recommended that he be taken to a mental hospital and be kept under a twenty-four-hour surveillance, because he is a very dangerous person, and he has very dangerous intentions in his head."

Matigari now turned abruptly and once again stood facing the Minister for Truth and Justice, the police chief, the judges, the Provincial Commissioner, the priest, Boy, Williams, the Permanent Professor of Parrotology and all the other dignitaries on the platform.

Youth seemed suddenly to come over him again. His voice sounded like thunder.

"The house is mine because I built it. The land is mine too because I tilled it with these hands. The industries are mine because my labor built and worked them. I shall never stop struggling for all the products of my sweat. I shed blood and I did not shed it in vain. One day the land will return to the tiller, and the wealth of our land to those who produce it. Poverty and sorrow shall be banished from our land!"

Matigari pointed at Robert Willams and John Boy Junior.

"And you, imperialist, and your servant Boy — with all your other lackeys, ministers and leaders of the police force, the army and the courts, the prisons and the administration — your days are numbered! I shall come back tomorrow. We are the patriots who survived: Matigari ma Njirũũngi! And many more of us are being born each day. John Boy, you shall not sleep in my house again. It's either you or me and the future belongs to me!"

People applauded.

The policemen hesitated for a while, but then they pounced on Matigari, handcuffed him and threw him into the darkness. The crowd booed. They all began singing:

Show me the way to a man
Whose name is Matigari ma Njirũũngi,
Who stamps his feet to the rhythm of bells.
And the bullets jingle.
And the bullets jingle.

The minister growled. He tried to raise his voice above the singing. He shouted:

"I have banned all the songs about Matigari ma Njirũũngi! I have also banned all dreams! This is a new law! Do you hear? All subversive songs and dreams are banned!"

The people continued singing. The police cocked their guns.

"The meeting is over!" the minister shouted. "Go home! You have all been dismissed!"

"And don't stop on the way! You are not allowed to walk in groups of more than five people," the police chief added.

But the people sang louder than ever before. Some started shouting for the release of Ngarũro wa Kĩrĩro. Others shouted slogans, "Down with theft and lies!"

"I have also banned crowds in the village," the Provincial Commissioner added. "I have authorized the chiefs to use their powers as provided by the Chiefs Act. They may arrest anyone found roaming about the village without sababu*."

The people rose as one and heaved towards the minister, still singing as though they wanted to go into the small room to free Matigari ma Njirũũngi, Ngarũro wa Kĩrĩro and all the other political prisoners.

The police commissioner blew his whistle. The police and the army came rushing in and drove the people out with the butts of their guns. People screamed and dashed out of the hall, heading for their homes. But as soon as they got to their places, they spoke of nothing else but Matigari ma Njirũũngi, Ngarũro wa Kĩrĩro and the brave university students.

"What?" asked those who had not been present.

"He said that the days of the imperialist robbers and their servant Boy are numbered."

"The forty days of a robber?"

"And when those days are over?"

---

*Sababu (Kiswahili): reason.

"Really! Must you have everything spelled out for you?"

"He will come back. He did not say exactly when, but he will surely come back."

"What a wonder! And his name?"

"Matigari ma Njirũũngi."

"It's quite true. Everything that has been said is true. There are two types of people in this country. There are those who sell out, and those who are patriots."

"Matigari ma Njirũũngi is a patriot."

18

In the mental hospital, Matigari ma Njirũũngi and Ngarũro wa Kĩrĩro talked nearly the whole night about the workers. . . peasants. . . freedom fighters. . . revolutionaries. . . about all the forces committed to building a new tomorrow for all our children. . . Amen.

They became like student and teacher. Each was both a student and a teacher to the other.

The birds began to sing:

If only it were dawn,
If only it were dawn,
So that I can share the cold waters with the early bird. . .

As they both slept, each in their respective beds, Gũthera and Mũriũki were agonising: *What can we do to help. . . ?*

19

No government, not even the most repressive, has ever managed to silence the voices of the masses. The songs spread like wildfire in a dry season. They spread through the villages. The people sang them day and night. They would start with the student's song:

Even if you kill us,
Victory belongs to the people.
Victory belongs to the people!

They would sing the song of Matigari ma Njirũũngi:

Show me the way to a man
Whose name is Matigari ma Njirũũngi
Who stamps his feet to the rhythm of bells.
And the bullets jingle.
And the bullets jingle.

But who *was* Matigari ma Njirũũngi?

❖

PART THREE

Gũthera na Mũriũki

❖

The Pure and the Resurrected

1

He made the decision while still in the mental hospital. It dawned on him that one could not defeat the enemy with arms alone, but one could also not defeat the enemy with words alone. One had to have the right words; but these words had to be strengthened by the force of arms. In the pursuit of truth and justice one had to be armed with armed words.

When the worker in metals returned from where he practiced his skill far away from home, and found an ogre starving his expectant wife, did he send the ogre peace greetings? Did he not first sharpen his spear?

Justice for the oppressed comes from a sharpened spear. He removed the belt of peace he had worn earlier and trampled it down on the ground.

2

The news was first heard at about 10 a.m. from the Voice of Truth. A group of patients had escaped from the mental hospital.

It was not known how they had managed to escape, but the police suspected that they had used a file to cut through the wire mesh that ran around the hospital.

The hospital administration was completely at a loss as to how the patients had obtained a file, for all instruments of violence such as sticks, razor blades and nails, or anything with a sharp edge, were prohibited. For the prisoners had to be protected from one another.

The police were still investigating, the radio announced. The government appealed to the public to be careful, because the madmen might be carrying dangerous objects.

The public were requested to keep listening to the radio. The police would continue giving reports about the progress made in tracking down the dangerous madmen.

3

. . . *This* is the Voice of Truth. . . *While waiting for more information on the escaped madmen, we have just received news that Britain and the European Community have given this country a loan of several million pounds for the development of the administration of instant justice. The loan will be used to buy hand-cuffs, hand and leg chains, uniforms for prison warders, electric fences to help guard the prisons and ropes for hanging those who have been sentenced to death. All the material must be bought from British factories or from the other EEC countries. Part of the loan will be used to send prison warders, high-court judges, riot police and district commissioners abroad for retraining in modern methods of the administration of instant justice. The Minister for Truth and Justice gave a vote of thanks. . . The United States government is requesting the World Bank and the IMF to give this country a loan for the development and the defense of the rule of law, truth and justice. . .*

The United States government has also said that it would be willing to listen with sympathy to a request to supply this country with Phantom jets, tanks and attack helicopters. The US government spokesman said this when he addressed Congress. He also thanked the government of this country for granting the USA military facilities at the coast. . .

4

When the priest heard the news about the escaped madmen, he fell on his knees and frantically began pleading with God. . . O Lord, you didn't give me a chance to visit those in the mental hospital. . . So if it should happen that you have come back among us disguised as a madman, remember, O Lord, that I was preparing to go there tomorrow. . .

5

This is the Voice of Truth. . . *A special announcement.
The police are continuing their search for a group of madmen who
escaped from a mental hospital. The policemen are also looking for
a woman and a boy, who were earlier seen taking food to one of
the patient. The police have appealed to the boy and woman to present themselves at the nearest police station, in order to help the
police in their investigations.*

6

This is the Voice of Truth. . . *This is another special police
announcement. . . The public are requested to report to the nearest police station anybody found speaking like a madman, or
dressed in rags like a madman, or anyone with unkempt hair like
a madman's or anybody seen asking awkward questions like a
madman, or doing things which only a madman would do. The
police are saying all those who are not mad must shave off their
beards, cut short their hair and keep it tidy at all times. They must
not, repeat must not, wear rags. . .*

7

It so happened that, when an elderly woman and her husband were rummaging through some dustbins, they came across
posters bearing the pictures of Jesus Christ and Karl Marx.

"Here are those lunatics we have been hearing so much
about!" the woman said to her husband.

"You are right there! They have long hair and long beards, just
like madmen!" the man exclaimed.

They each carried a picture and headed for the nearest police
station.*" Nyinyi wenda wazimu!"* the policemen shouted.* "We
want the actual madmen — not their photographs! Go and bring
those madmen; or better still, take us to where they are. . ."

Nyinyi wenda wazimu (Kiswahili): "you must be mad."

8

. . . This is the Voice of Truth. . . This is an urgent announcement. . . The Minister for Truth and Justice has authorized the police to shoot down all madmen. . . Shoot on sight!. . .

9

The police have set up road-blocks on all the roads in their continued efforts to arrest the escaped madmen. Many vehicles, especially buses and matatus, *have been searched. It is believed that some of the madmen might use public transport to escape. The police have asked the drivers and conductors of matatus and buses to report anyone with no bus fare, as it is believed that these madmen have no money on them. Other road users have been instructed to report anybody seen hitching a lift. . .*

10

. . . This is the Voice of Truth. . . The police have been told not to harass white people even if they are wearing long beards and have unkempt hair or even if they are dressed in rags and dirty clothes, or are hitching lifts, or are without bus fare. The police made this announcement after the United States, and British Governments complained through their embassies here that their citizens are being harassed on the roads in the belief that they are madmen, merely because of their beards and their long, unkempt hair. The Minister for Truth and Justice apologized and warned people against racism. The public were warned against finding fault in people because of their white color. The chief of police has told the police and members of the public that, in any case, white people do not go mad. The police would like to inform the public that the escaped madmen, with the exception of one Asian, are all black. . .

11

This is a special announcement. . . *This is a special announcement. . . The police have shot one of the escaped madmen. He has been identified as Ngarūro wa Kīrĩro. He was rushed into hospital in a critical condition. Before he was shot down, he demonstrated violent tendencies and boasted how he was going to make the rest of the workers mad. He even tried to influence the security forces, by telling them that they too were workers and that they were being used by the government of capitalists, landlords and imperialists as watchdogs. . .*

12

. . . A special announcement. . . The police have revealed that one of the escaped madmen is the one who calls himself Matigari ma Njirũũngi. The public are warned that this man is particularly dangerous because he has delusions that everything belongs to him: houses, the land, the industries and even all the women. This is the second time this week that this madman has slipped through the fingers of the law. The first time was after he had been arrested on Mr. John Boy Junior's land. He demanded the keys to his house by force. It is still not known how he managed to break out and escape from the cell. He was taken to the mental hospital yesterday after shouting down the Minister for Truth and Justice. The Minister was speaking at a meeting held to resolve a dispute between striking workers and their employers. The police are still investigating how a woman and a boy were allowed to take him food after the court had ordered twenty-four-hour surveillance over him. The police are still waiting for the woman and boy to appear and assist them. Police have also been sent to guard John Boy Junior's home. . . and John Boy Junior has been assigned body-guards to protect him from Matigari ma Njirũũngi. . .

13

At the time Matigari, Gũthera and Mũriũki were sitting under a *leleshwa* bush trying in vain to keep cool under the little shade of its leafless branches. The sun was blazing, hotter than the hottest coals, and scorched them mercilessly. The grass withered and wilted in the heat.

"This scorching sun makes the heat of the day before yesterday feel like ice by comparison," Gũthera said.

"Yes, and yesterday was such a lifeless day," Mũriũki said in response. "It was neither hot nor cold."

"This kind of heat harbors ill," she added.

Matigari lay on his back. He used his coat to support his head. He covered his face with his hat. His snoring was like the roar of a lion in the wilderness. Gũthera and Mũriũki were just sitting on the grass. Gũthera wore a *lasso* of white and black print, with patterns all over it. She wore this round her shoulders. Mũriũki's clothes were still covered with patches of all the colors of the rainbow.

"Let's wake him up," Gũthera said; but by the time she had finished the sentence, Matigari was already fully awake.

"Let's go," he said. His voice did not betray the fact that he had just woken up.

"But where are we going?" asked Mũriũki.

"To the house!" Matigari answered him.

Mũriũki and Gũthera exchanged glances. He still wanted to go back to the house that had got him into all these problems?

"Isn't it better for you to leave those people alone?" Gũthera asked. "Yes, isn't it much better for you to stop asking too many questions, better for you to forget the house and save your life? Seal your lips?"

"You mean that I should seal my life in a tomb of silence? That I should abandon all the produce of my head and hands? Leave everything to parasites? The labor of he-who-sows to them-who-never-sow? Listen to me, Gũthera. This world is upside-down, but it must be set right again. For I have seen that in our land today lies are decreed to be the truth, and the truth is decreed to be a lie. Theft and corruption have become the order of the day. That is what people pride themselves on. Should the shepherd and the shepherdess let the wolves and hyenas herd their sheep for them? This world is indeed upside-down, and it must be set to rights again. The builder wants a place in which to lay his head. The tiller wants his harvest. The worker wants the produce of his labor. We have refused to be the cooking pot that just cooks and never tastes the food. Or do you want our women to continue trading their bodies for a few coins? Our children too, do you want them to continue scavenging in dustbins for left-overs, like vultures? Boy will never sleep in my house again."

"Supposing they arrest you again, and take you back to prison, or to the mental hospital? They might even do something worse to you."

"Let me tell you one thing," Matigari said. "Whether they imprison, detain or kill us, they will never stop we who toil from struggling against those who only feed on our toil. Between producers and parasites, there will never be peace, or unity, or love. Never! Supposing our forefathers and foremothers had behaved as if they had no eyes to see, no ears to hear and no tongues to speak? Where then would we be today? Yesterday, yes only yesterday, I believed that if I wore a belt of peace, I would be able to find truth and justice in this country. For it has been said that truth and justice are mightier than any armed power. That the enemy who is driven out peacefully, by negotiations, never comes back. But the one driven out by force alone always comes back. Yet where did that kind of thinking land me? First in prison, then in the mental hospital. If it were not for the two of you, where would I be today? Still in prison, or in a mental hospital. Since last night, I have now learned a new lesson — or, rather, learned a new and an old lesson. The enemy can never be driven out by words alone, no matter how sound the argument. Nor can the enemy be driven out by force alone. But words of truth and justice, fully backed by armed power, will certainly drive the enemy out. When right and might are on the same side, what enemy can hold out? In a wilderness dominated by beasts of prey, or in a market run by thieves, robbers and murderers, justice can come only from the armed force of the united oppressed. Boy will never again sleep in my house for as long as I live."

"And from where will you get your armed forces?" Mūriūki asked him.

Matigari looked at both Gūthera and Mūriūki for a while. He told them the same story of how he came out from the forest, armed with an AK47, a pistol, a sword and a cartridge belt. He also told them of how he had hidden them under a *mūgumo* tree.

"How does the saying go? You may well return to places you once left behind. What shall I add to that? You may well return to find an unfinished war. I will retrace my steps to where I went astray and resume my journey from there. It is better to build another house altogether — a new house with a better foundation. But what I know for sure is that, for as long as I am alive, I shall never allow Boy to inherit my house."

"Let's go! Let's go and get the gun now!" Mũriũki said excitedly, already imagining himself wearing a gun.

"No," said Matigari. "I don't want you to lose your lives before your time has come. Let us say goodbye to one another here. I shall go and recover my weapons from under the tree. Then I shall claim my house with new might and right."

"Please let me come!" Mũriũki begged. "Don't leave me behind."

"I will come too," Gũthera said. "One can die only once, and it is better to die in pursuit of what is right."

"Yes. We are the children of Matigari ma Njirũũngi," Mũriũki said. "We are the children of the patriots who survived the war."

"And their wives as well!" said Gũthera, smiling. "Or which other wives and children were you looking for?" She was silent for a while. Then she started talking in a subdued tone about the thoughts which bothered her.

"From the moment you saved me from the dogs of prey, I have felt very discontented. Yes, I have not been satisfied with the kind of life I have been leading. You see, my entire life has been dominated by men, be they our Father in heaven, my father on earth, the priest or all the men who have bought my body and turned me into their mattress.

"What I really want to say is that most of the things I have been doing so far have not sprung from my being able to choose.

"I have been wearing blinkers like a horse. Yes, I have never done anything which came from free choice. I've been moved here and there by time and place. Except yesterday when I broke my eleventh commandment. I could have chosen not to do it, but I didn't. I chose to do it freely for an end in which I believed.

"But that is not what I really want to say. You see, I have known all along that the life I have been leading is not that of a human being. It has been more like that of an animal. . . my life has not been any different from that of any animal, which breathes, eats, drinks and goes to sleep. Therefore, the most important thing is not just to know that my life has been without meaning. I would say that there is no woman who does not really know the pressures that we women live under.

"What is troubling my thoughts is this. Once a person knows, what does she do about it? Or is knowing just good in itself? Is it enough for me just to say that now I know? I want to do something to change whatever it is that makes people live like animals, especially us women. What can we as women do to change our lives? Or will we continue to follow the paths carved out for us by men? Aren't we in the majority anyway? Let's go! From now on, I want to be among the vanguard. I shall never be left behind again. Matigari, stamp your feet to the rhythm and let the bullets tinkle! May our fears disappear with the staccato sound of our guns!"

Matigari bent his head and turned his face away. He felt hot tears sting his eyelids.

"Let us go now!" he said in an unsteady voice, as though holding back the tears with difficulty. *"Saying is doing* is our motto."

Just then they heard the purring of an engine. They looked at one another.

Cars in the plains? In this wilderness?

14

"We can't be far from the road that we passed, then?" Gûthera asked.

"Mûriûki, why don't you climb up that tree and see what it is," Matigari said.

Mûriûki climbed up the tree. There was no road in sight. But, true, there was a car in the wilderness. It drove at a snail's pace. Then it stopped by a small cluster of *leleshwa* bushes some distance from where they were.

"It's a Mercedes! It's a Mercedes-Benz!" Mûriûki exclaimed. "It's stopped."

Matigari and Gûthera crept out of the ditch. They looked across at the car. It was indeed a black Mercedes. They waited for the occupants of the car to come out.

Far beyond the Mercedes, one could see a flock of sheep and a herd of cattle grazing. Other than these, and the black Mercedes, the plain stretched endlessly and lifelessly under the sun.

"What are they eating in this hot sun?" Gũthera asked, pointing at the animals.

"You ought to have asked what the shepherds are eating in this hot sun."

"Milk comes from cows, and the cows from the grass, and so if the animals have nothing to eat, it means that the people will have nothing to drink. So if I ask about the cow, I am at the same time asking about the shepherd."

Matigari looked at Gũthera and said, "You have a point there."

"There is a great difference between human beings and animals," Gũthera added as if struck by a new thought. "Human beings can store food in granaries and in this way, they should not starve. That means that people starve only because they choose to."

Matigari looked at Gũthera as though seeing her for the first time.

"You have a point there," he repeated.

"The problem here is that the surplus from many hands remains in the hands of some parasites. They sell the people's food to fatten their own bank accounts. The fool's staff is used by the cunning," Gũthera said. "It's only now that I begin to see what it is you have been struggling for all this time."

The occupants of the car remained inside. Matigari called to Mũriũki:

"Come down from that tree."

Mũriũki came back to them.

"Just walk slowly towards that car and pretend to be a shepherd boy. See what they are doing there. Caution is not a sign of cowardice. Then find a way of getting back here without letting whoever is in the car see you."

Mũriũki looked around for a stick. He pitched it across his shoulder and held each end with one hand, just like shepherd boys do.

"Where did you learn to do that? Were you once a shepherd boy?" Gũthera asked him, laughing.

"No, I am just imitating what I've seen shepherd boys do."

"If anything happens to prevent us from meeting again," Matigari said, "make your way to the house this evening."

Mũriũki left them still lying on their stomachs, looking across at the Mercedes.

"Maybe those are ivory poachers," Gũthera said.

"What use could they possibly have for ivory? You can't eat ivory!"

"You have really been gone for a long time," Gũthera said, laughing. This morning Gũthera was in a really good mood. "Of course they sell it. What did you say about food? They convert it into fat checks. The same applies to ivory. They work with some greedy Asians and some greedy Europeans."

"Don't they know that animals are man's friends? When we were in the forest we never killed any animals at any cost unless we were hungry and had run out of food. Even when we came across an injured animal, we would mend their broken limbs. Animals were very useful to us. They used to warn us when there was imminent danger. You know that there are ways of talking with animals. If you stay in the forests and mountains for a long time, you get to learn how to talk to them. Sometimes the animals talk to you. You just remain silent, listening to them. How do you think that shepherds like those ones there survive out here on the plains? They have forged special ties with the animals."

"These Mercedes people only shepherd money taken from the workers," Gũthera said.

They saw Mũriũki approaching the Mercedes. He walked past the car and a little beyond it.

"How come the driver has not come out even to relieve himself?" Gũthera asked.

"Who told you that drivers always need to relieve themselves?"

"How is it you are so quick to come in the defense of drivers? Were you ever a driver?"

"Who, me? There is no job that these hands of mine have not done for the settler."

They saw Mũriũki making his way back. They waited. He was smiling slyly.

"Who is it?" Gũthera asked.

"It's a couple," Mũriũki said, trying his best not to laugh.

"Why, what are they doing?"

Now Mũriũki burst out laughing. Gũthera looked at Matigari, whose expression had not changed.

"They are doing love. They have no clothes on. They have turned the radio on, but they are not listening to it."

"Leave them alone. Let's go away." Matigari said.

"But where will we pass?" Mũriũki asked.

"Why?" Gũthera asked in turn.

"I heard the radio announce that the police have set up road-blocks on all major roads. It also announced that anyone who sees a man, a boy and a woman together should report them immediately to the police."

"So we are surrounded?" Gũthera asked.

"It looks like it," Matigari said, deep in thought. A crease appeared on his forehead.

"To get to the *mũgumo* tree, we have to pass through many roads, and we have to pass many people. We might get arrested before we get there."

"Or before we get to the house," Gũthera added.

"I have sworn that Boy cannot sleep in that house another night. He and I cannot share the same roof," Matigari said, pained at the implication of Gũthera's words.

"What shall we do?" she asked.

"If we can find a bus or a *matatu*, we can first go to the children's village and hide there until nightfall. Then we can go to the *mũgumo* tree, take the guns and take the sword, go to the house and tell Boy and Williams: *Hands up! Surrender!"*

"You mean that the children will house us in their cars?" Gũthera asked, laughing.

"Of course! They would like nothing better than just to shake Matigari's hand. You see, ever since they threw stones at him, they have been wondering what they can do to undo the wrong they did. It was only yesterday that they were asking me: What can we do to help Matigari? Most of them are now calling themselves Matigari ma Njirũũngi. They even thought of taking something to Matigari to help him escape from the mental hospital."

"Is that where you picked the idea up from?" Gũthera asked Mũriũki. "What wonderful children! The patriots who survived the war," Gũthera said quietly.

Matigari was staring into space. He looked as if he were not listening to what they were saying.

"That's not a bad idea!" he said suddenly.

"You mean going to the children's village? Or you mean going to look for a bus or a *matatu*?" Gũthera asked him.

"If we travel by bus or by *matatu*, or even go to the children's village, we will be hiding right under their noses as it were. It is usually easy to hide in obvious places. Most people don't see what is right under their noses."

"But buses and *matatus* are being searched," said Gũthera.

"We'll find our own *matatu*," Matigari said, getting up at the same time. "We'd better get moving now."

They followed Matigari across the plains towards the Mercedes. Matigari's intentions suddenly dawned on them.

Mũriũki was beside himself with excitement.

"A Mercedes-Benz! To become a *matatu!*"

15

The man and woman lay naked in the back seat of the car. The ignition keys were still in the starter. They seemed to think that nobody would be needing the car keys here in the wilderness. Nobody would be after their Mercedes here in the wilderness. . .

Matigari left them their underwear only, saying, "If you talk about this before tomorrow, I shall park the car by the roadside and display your clothes in such a way that everyone will know what you were doing in the wilderness. But if you promise not to tell anybody about it, I shall leave the car in a safe place and burn your clothes to destroy all the evidence of what you were doing. You can do what you like with yourselves. It is not important to me. That is a matter between the two of you. So make up your minds whether you want this incident to remain secret, or whether you want the whole world to know."

Gũthera and Mũriũki sat in the back seat, each in their own corner. Matigari took the wheel.

"I seem to have seen that woman somewhere," Gũthera remarked, after they had driven for a short distance.

"Some faces remind you of other faces," Matigari said in a matter-of-fact way. "The human race has the same roots, you know. It's only that they have been dispersed by time and space into different camps."

Gũthera remained silent. She was not satisfied with this explanation. The woman's face kept flashing in her mind.

The Mercedes was one of the latest models. It had an air-conditioner. It was also an automatic and they could open or close the windows by just pressing a button. The windows had blinds across them.

Behind the front seat was a little bar. Mũriũki pressed a button, and a light came on. The little door opened and a row of glasses appeared arranged in the bar. There were different types of drinks there: Chivas Regal, Gordon's Dry Gin, Bristol Cream sherry, green Chartreuse and Dom Perignon, as well as some soda water, ginger ale and Coca-Cola.

"It's just like a house!" Gũthera exclaimed. "A bar in a car with all sorts of drinks! Blinds across the windows, and reclining seats, just like beds! A stereo recorder and radio too."

Mũriũki opened a bottle of Coca-Cola with his teeth. He made himself comfortable in his corner and started drinking the Coke, sipping a little at a time.

"Where is this cool air coming from?" he asked.

"From the fan. The car has an air-conditioner," Gũthera informed him.

The car glided along the tarmac road. They felt no bumps, no pot-holes; the car absorbed all these.

Mũriũki could not keep still. He touched this and that or looked out of the window at other people and at other cars.

"Look! Horses! Horses!" he shouted.

"Oh, those ones? Those are the racehorses," Gũthera explained to him.

"Is that where all the people in all these cars are going?"

"Yes."

The entrance to the racecourse was close to the road. There was a signpost with "CITY JOCKEY CLUB. NOW OPEN FOR ALL RACES" boldly written on it.

"There are Africans and Asians too?"

"Yes."

They drove along the fence of the racecourse. On the other side of the road was a hangar, and just behind it -

"Airplanes! Airplanes! Look at those little airplanes!" Mũriũki exclaimed.

"These are planes for tourists and business men," Gũthera told him. "Rich Americans and Europeans come here to hire them."

"What about the big airplanes? Where are they?"

"Those are at the international airport."

"Do African people hire the planes too?"

"Oh, yes! Some do! You know, people like Boy. Money is all you need to hire one."

"I've just had an idea!" Mūriūki suddenly said. "Let's go and steal one of those small airplanes and fly it to the *mūgumo* tree."

Gūthera laughed.

They drove through the center of the capital city. They drove through the main street.

"Long ago, this road was named after a governor, you know, those colonial ones," Gūthera told Mūriūki. "But now it is named after His Excellency Ole Excellence. All the roads which were named after the governors or kings or queens during the colonial days are now named after His Excellency."

"He is our governor," Mūriūki said. Then after a little while he asked, "Why isn't Ole Excellence called King? King Excellence!"

"I don't know."

On either side of the highway they were now driving on were tall buildings. Neon lights flashed their various names: American Express, Citibank, Barclays, Bank of Japan, American Life, Inter-Continental, The Hilton, Woolworth's, Wimpy Bar, Kentucky Fried Chicken, McDonalds, Shah's Supermarket Stores, Bata Shoes, African Retailers and many others. The neon lights seemed to be competing for attention.

"Have you ever been here before?" Mūriūki asked Gūthera.

"Oh, yes. Many times."

"This is my first time," he said.

When they got to the industrial area of the city, Gūthera said, "I've never been to this part of the city before." She continued glancing out through the window, and she read out the different names as they flashed by. "General Motors . . . Firestone . . . Coca-Cola . . . IBM . . . Unilever Products . . . Madhvani Products . . . Del Monte . . . BAT . . . Union Carbide . . . Mitsubishi Products . . . African Cycle Mart . . ." and so on. Then she got tired and turned her thoughts to the woman. Where had she seen her before?

They went past some workers' houses. These were many tiny houses crammed together. They drove past estate after estate. The walls were as black as soot. Not a single plant graced their yards. Pedestrians, buses, cars, cyclists and a few carts all competed for the use of the road.

Then they came to the place where the rich lived, and Mūriūki thought that these were the houses that he had often seen in a

National Geographic magazine which he had found in a dustbin.
He had stuck these photographs on the walls of his Mercedes-
Benz house. The houses they were driving past were large, with
huge gardens. There were flowered lawns and green trees everywhere. At the entrances stood huge steel gates. From the road one
could see swimming-pools full of clear blue water. Despite the
drought in the country, these homes had enough water for their
lawns and shrubs and their swimming-pools. At each gate there
was a security guard with an Alsatian dog and a sign: *"Mbwa
Kali."*

"It is true that there are two worlds here in this country,"
Gũthera said, as though she was reading Mũriũki's thoughts.

The drive was so smooth. Each time they came across a road-
block the police would wave them by. In some cases the policemen would move the road-blocks so that the Mercedes could get
through more easily, without the set-back of slowing down.

Mũriũki felt like opening the window and showing his face to
the policemen. He felt like telling them, "It's us you're looking
for!" or, "This is Matigari ma Njirũũngi." How he would have loved
to see the look on their faces then!

"This Mercedes-Benz is like a ticket to heaven!" he said happily.

He stared across at the trees, which seemed to be retreating
in the direction opposite the one they were driving in.

Gũthera was deep in thought. The image of the woman kept
on coming back to her. She now lifted the clothes and admired
them, especially the woman's dress. They were expensive. She
opened the handbag, and something fell out. It was a photograph.

"I know who she is!" she exclaimed.

"Who is she?" Mũriũki asked.

"This is a photo of her!"

"Of who?"

"The woman in the car. She is the wife of the Minister for Truth
and Justice."

"How do you know?"

"I've seen her photograph in the papers. She always appears
on telly, and she is always in the papers. Who wouldn't recognize
her? You should hear her on the radio talking about the role of
women. She is a fine one to talk! She tells people how women

Mbwa Kali (Kiswahili): "Beware. Dogs Within" — literally, "dangerous dogs."

should live in the home: *Women are the corner-stones of the home.* That is her favorite tune. She even once said that all barmaids and all prostitutes should be locked up in prison because they are the ones who were causing a lot of homes to break up. And now there she is — stark naked in the wilderness! She never fails going to church! She goes to the cathedrals; she usually burns a golden candle. . ."

"This world is upside down," Matigari suddenly said. "The robber calls the robbed *robber.* The murderer calls the murdered *murderer,* and the wicked calls the righteous *evil.* The one uprooting evil is accused of planting evil. The seeker of truth and justice ends up in prisons and detention camps. Yes, those who sow good seeds are accused of sowing weeds. As for the sell-outs, they are too busy locking up our patriots in gaols, or sending them into exile to let outsiders come and bask in the comfort wrought by others. Those we have left in the wilderness are not the only ones doing evil. Yes, this world is upside-down. Those to whom it belongs must set it to rights again!"

"When she gets home, whatever will she say?" Gũthera asked, her thoughts still on the woman. No one answered her.

They drove in silence. Each was preoccupied by their own thoughts. Each time Mũriũki shut his eyes, he saw the frame of his Mercedes-Benz take to life and fly like an aeroplane or gallop like a horse. He was in turn the driver and the rider. Matigari was planning how he would take up arms to fight for his house yet again. The failure of one crop does not deter one from sowing seeds again. Gũthera was still deeply engrossed in her thoughts. She kept on thinking about the woman, feeling very sorry for her. What problems we women have to go through wherever we are! When that woman goes home, her husband will beat her, demanding to know what she was doing in the wilderness with a man. When her lover goes home, he will beat his wife for demanding to know what he was doing in the wilderness with a woman.

Matigari now turned on the radio. After a bit of soft music, the news came on.

. . . *USA has rejected the recent proposals by the Soviet Union for the elimination of all nuclear weapons on earth* . . . USA has*

---

*This was written in 1983, a few years before Reykjavik.

decided to militarize space. . . USA and Soviet Union have launched
more spaceships. . .

"They are forever reporting on the USA and the Soviet Union!"
Gũthera exclaimed.

"And also His Excellency!" Mũriũki remarked. "Just wait, listen!" But for a time, the radio did not mention His Excellency, Ole
Excellence. Gũthera laughed.

   . . . Guerrillas in El Salvador have blown up a railway bridge
in the capital city. They said that they will never relinquish their
arms until the USA and its lackeys in El Salvador accept the demo-
cratic process. . . Local News: Reports say that His Excellency Ole
Excellence. . .

"I told you! I told you!" Mũriũki cried out triumphantly, glad
that he had been proved right. Gũthera and Mũriũki burst out
laughing. Their laughter was short lived.

   . . . As you may have heard in the news earlier, one of the mad-
men, Ngarũro wa Kĩrĩro, died earlier today in hospital after being
shot. . . Ngarũro was shot down by police after threatening them
with violence —

"God! No!" Gũthera exclaimed.

They went on in silence.

They drove through huge coffee, tea, sisal and pineapple plantations. Later they went past narrow strips of land which were
parched and over-utilized.

Matigari spoke again.

"There are indeed two worlds," he said, as though echoing
Gũthera's words. "The world of patriots and that of sell-outs."

They came to a golf course. Endless lawns could be seen, with
jets of water streaming from fountains, watering the grass in mock
defiance of the sun.

"If there was famine, would people eat this coffee, or this tea,
or these lawns?" Gũthera sadly yet bitterly asked.

"We are nearly there!" Matigari announced. "This golf course
was there in the days of Settler Williams and John Boy."

"And it is still here today in these times of Robert Williams and John Boy Junior," Gũthera replied.

"Surrender!" shouted Mũriũki, still dreaming of a gunfight.

"We must work out how we are going to get to the children's village without being seen," Matigari said.

"We should go one by one," Gũthera suggested. "I'll drop off here, and I will see you there later."

She got off between the gate to the factory and the road leading to the market.

Mũriũki and Matigari drove on. Mũriũki dropped off, leaving all the joy and comfort of the Mercedes behind.

Matigari drove on alone, in search of a parking space. "The best way to hide something is to leave it right under the nose of those looking for it," he said again to himself.

He suddenly remembered the Esso petrol-station he had seen earlier, next to the Sheraton Hotel, and drove towards it.

All the cars parked there were Mercedes-Benzes. Matigari found a space and squeezed the car into it. He opened the boot and put the clothes, shoes and handbag in it. He put the keys in his pocket.

He first walked towards the factory. When he got to the spot where he had met Ngarũro for the first time, Matigari took his hat and stood there for a minute or two.

Before he got to the road, he heard two raised voices, talking as if they intended him to hear what they were saying.

"Did you listen to the news?"

"What news? That His Excellency visited some school or other, or that he received some donation, or that he has warned people against rumor-mongering, or that he has paid some place a visit? His Excellency here, His Excellency there, His Excellency everywhere! I am tired of all that! I don't listen to the radio any more!"

"Jesus will find you asleep. . . when he returns."

"Look, if you have nothing better to talk about, don't talk to me about Jesus."

"You know the minister's wife? The Minister for Truth and Justice? She and her driver were attacked by thieves, who stole their car."

"Really?"

"I hear that they were going to the races. . . to see the horses which this woman bought jointly with the Aga Khan compete. . . "

"So African people do own racing horses?"

"*Maendeleo ya muafirika, maendeleo ya wanawake. . .* And that is not the end of the story. I hear that the thieves were armed to the teeth."

Matigari controlled his laughter with difficulty. He crossed the road.

Just wait till the night falls. I will get my AK47 from under the *mũgumo* tree, Matigari said to himself, and then they will see me truly armed to the teeth.

16

By the time Matigari got there, Mũriũki had already told the other children everything except about the guns. So the children did not clap or cheer, nor did they jump up and down for joy, for fear of drawing the attention of passers-by. But despite their efforts not to draw people's attention, they could not hide the admiration they felt for him.

Matigari went into one of the cars, a Peugeot model. Gũthera went into a wreck of a Ford, and Mũriũki went to his Mercedes Benz. They were all very tired. It was a very hot day. They slept.

The children kept guard. They arranged themselves so that some were strategically placed on the road, others at the shopping center and others in the restaurants. They agreed that whoever saw the police would rush and inform the others, or whistle a signal to warn the others. Those who were left behind were to collect heaps of stones. These were for defense, in case the police came to invade their village. They would defend the three while they slept. They were spoiling for a fight. Some of them started making catapults and slings.

They turned on the radio and listened to some music. This was followed by a religious program. It was run by an American priest, of the Jesus Is My Savior sect. This was followed by the news.

Maendeleo ya muafirika, maendeleo ya wanawake (Kiswahili): "African people's progress, women's progress."

. . . An American nuclear carrier has called at the port on the coast of. . . about ten thousand Marines are said to have come ashore for rest and recuperation. . . The ships have sailed from South Africa, heading for the Middle East. The mayor of the town and all his councillors paid a visit to the carrier. In his address to the officers, the mayor thanked the marines for the foreign exchange they would bring to the town . . The tradesmen in the town are reported to have sold a lot of condoms.

Reports from the town say that a girl has been repeatedly stabbed with a bottle by her lover, an American Marine. She died on the spot.

"How comes it that these Americans are all over the world?" one of the boys asked.

"Let's listen to music on the other channel," another said.

Gũthera and Matigari were startled from their sleep by Mũriũki's screams. The other children also came running to see what was going on.

"I was dreaming that I was in an airplane," he said. "But then it was not an airplane, it was a Mercedes-Benz. Then it changed into a winged house. Then I saw two birds come in through the window. But they weren't exactly birds. It was a man and a woman — they had no clothes on. . . Then I saw Gũthera and Matigari. They were bleeding from head to toe."

Gũthera shuddered.

"It is getting late," she said casually. "The sun has already set, hasn't it? Have any policemen been around?"

"No!"

"Why didn't you wake us up?" Matigari asked, and he started preparing as if to leave. 'We had better go before it gets dark," he said to Gũthera.

The children stood around Matigari. They were all very curious. They touched his clothes. Then they told him what was happening. From their story, he gathered that everybody was heading in the direction of the house.

"Which house?"

"Oh, Boy's!" one of the boys said.

"To the house!" another added.

"But what are they going there for?" Gũthera asked.

"Rumor has it that Matigari will return today, because it was only this morning that the Angel Gabriel, the same one who let him out of prison, let him out of the mental hospital. There will be a lot of policemen there too."

"Some people started going there long before you two got here," another boy said.

"They want to see a miracle!" said another.

"Some people have posters with slogans 'Expect a Miracle'. "Will you be going there?"

"Yes, I will," Matigari answered.

"We are coming too," they all said together.

"Tell us, are you the one whose Second Coming is prophesied?" asked one of the boys.

"Jesus Christ? The Lord who will bring the New Jerusalem here on earth?" added another.

Matigari hesitated for a little while. He looked at the children. Then his glance went beyond them to the car wreckage, and beyond those to the mountains.

"No," he answered them. "The God who is prophesied is in you, in me and in the other humans. He has always been there inside us since the beginning of time. Imperialism has tried to kill that God within us. But one day that God will return from the dead. Yes, one day that God within us will come alive and liberate us who believe in Him. I am not dreaming.

"He will return on the day when His followers will be able to stand up without worrying about tribe, race or color, and say in one voice: Our labor produced all the wealth in this land. So from today onwards we refuse to sleep out in the cold, to walk about in rags, to go to bed on empty bellies. Let the earth return to those to whom it belongs. Let the soil return to the tiller, the factory to the worker. . . But that God lives more in you children of this land; and therefore if you let the country go to the imperialist enemy and its local watchdogs, it is the same thing as killing that God who is inside you. It is the same thing as stopping Him from resurrecting. That God will come back only when you want Him to."

The children looked at one another in surprise. Matigari spoke in an even voice, but his words touched their very souls. He spoke as though he could read into their very hearts.

Matigari, Gũthera and Mũriũki went a little distance away from the children and whispered together. They discussed what they were going to do next. Matigari came up with an idea.

"Since there are a lot of people at the house now, this is what I have decided to do. You go to the house, with the rest of the children. I shall go and check if that Mercedes is where I left it. I shall drive to the *mũgumo* tree, where I shall arm myself and then come and join you. Right now, I am not afraid of dying for the just cause — our heritage!"

"Supposing the Mercedes isn't there?" Gũthera asked.

"Don't worry. I will still come to the house." he said. "What did I tell you? Boy will never sleep in my house again. He and I cannot both sleep in the same house tonight. I would rather build a new house altogether from scratch — a bigger house, a house with proper foundations, a firm foundation!"

"You had better hurry, then," Gũthera said.

"And bring me a pistol!" Mũriũki added. He was still thinking of cowboy films.

Matigari went away, leaving them all staring after him.

Gũthera and Mũriũki disappeared among the children as they streamed with everyone else in the direction of the house where they would all witness a miracle.

17

It was true that everyone was expecting a miracle on that day. Soldiers and policemen were everywhere. They wanted to catch Matigari alive or dead but in the presence of the crowd. That would quell all the rumors about miracles, angels and Christ's Second Coming. "People must be allowed to see it all," were the instructions of the police chief.

Robert Williams' house where John Boy had gone to hide was heavily guarded. Boy sat very close to the telephone so that he could be the first to get the welcome news of Matigari's arrest or death. And so, like everybody else, the two, Williams and Boy, anxiously waited for a miracle.

News editors waited.

Radio reporters waited.

Television crews had brought all their equipment to the scene. They waited.

The whole country waited.

They all shared the same hope: that a miracle should take place. But at the same time all wondered: who really *was* Matigari ma Njirũũngi? A patriot? Angel Gabriel? Jesus Christ? Was he a human being or a spirit? A true or false prophet? A savior or simply a lunatic? Was Matigari a man or was he a woman? A child or an adult? Or was he only an idea, an image, in people's minds? *Who Was He?*

People from all religions and denominations continued streaming towards the house. They carried Bibles, crosses, Korans, rosaries of all sizes and colors. They sang and beat drums. They all waited for Jehovah's sword to fall from heaven. . . the Final Judgment. . .

Whatever the whispers of doubt, it was better to be on the safe side, just in case. . .

18

Matigari hurried towards the Esso filling-station where he had parked the Mercedes.

Suddenly, he stopped in his tracks. Except for the minister's car, not another Mercedes was in sight, nor any other model for that matter. Was this a trap perhaps? He looked around him, thinking that there might be a policeman somewhere. He saw no one.

He walked to the petrol-station and asked for some fuel in a jerrycan. All the while, he kept on casting surreptitious glances around.

In the inner office sat a man smoking a cigarette. Matigari could not see his face clearly.

"Where have all the cars gone to?" Matigari asked the forecourt attendant.

"Haven't you heard?"

"What?"

"The whole country has gone to Boy's house."

"Is there a party there or something?"

"Do you mean to say that you really haven't heard the news?"

"What news?"

"People believe that a man called Matigari ma Njirũũngi who escaped from the mental hospital this morning might be trying to get into Boy's house by force. The police want to catch him alive in front of everybody. If you ask me, I would say that the man is not crazy."

"Why? What is he like?"

"Some people say this, and others say that. Some say that he is as tall as a giant, and that his head touches the sky. Others say that he is as little as a dwarf. Some say that Matigari is a woman, and others maintain that he is a man. Some people think that he is an adult, and others that he or she is a child. Nobody knows what nationality he derives from. It is rumored that he speaks many different languages. I have heard people say that he is a solitary person, but then others say that he is always led by a boy and followed by a woman. You might see him this minute, then all of a sudden he is nowhere to be seen. All you see is a woman and a boy. He is here, he is there, he is everywhere. You never know what to believe. If it were not for these foreign-owned companies that we work for, I would be there."

Matigari paid for the petrol and walked towards the Mercedes. Before opening the car door, he turned around. He saw the man he had earlier seen smoking a cigarette leave the office. Their eyes met. It was Gĩcerũ, the informer, the man he had been to prison with — the same man with whom he had shared a cell.

Matigari saw him speaking with the garage attendant. Then both men turned towards the car.

Matigari made a quick calculation. There was no other car in sight. So the only other possibility for the informer was to telephone. He reached a quick decision. He got into the car, started the engine and drove off.

The informer could do as he pleased. Death comes but once! Gĩcerũ made for the telephone.

19

He took the main road. There was still a hint of daylight, although the sun had set. He pressed harder on the accelerator, and the car leaped forward. Matigari wondered whether he should first go to the house if only to see the people who were gathered

there. He resisted the temptation. Justice for the oppressed springs
from the organized armed power of the people. Matigari had
already laid down the belt of peace. He would now return to the
forests and the mountains and wear his belt of arms for a second
struggle. To whom would his people otherwise turn? How could
he continue sweating, only for the breed of parasites to reap where
they had not sown? When, oh when, would that day come when;

> The builder shall live in a decent house,
> The tailor wear decent clothes,
> The tiller eat a decent meal?
> No, the producer refuses to produce for parasites to harvest.
> We the toilers refuse to be the pot that cooks but never eats the
>   food.
> Every human being has a pair of hands.

The words formed into a song in his head. He sang it over
and over again.

As he sang the song, he recalled the talk he had had with
Ngarũro wa Kĩrĩro. Ngarũro had told him that there were two camps
in the country. There was that of the imperialists and their retinue
of messengers, overseers, police and military. The ruling party
were these messengers, and they had control over the government, the laws and the gunmen in boots. The ideas and the culture and the history they cultivated in the land were those singing
glory to the role of carrying messages. . . On the other hand, there
was the camp of the working people, with their values, their culture and their history. The ruling party of messengers was trying
to imprison the real history of the working people behind bars
and in detention camps. For how long, Ngarũro had cried, were
we going to endure this rule by messengers and overseers?

Justice for the oppressed, Matigari had told him; yes, justice
for the oppressed springs from the armed might of the united dispossessed!. . .

He glanced in the rear-view mirror. Behind him was a police
car. He stepped harder on the accelerator. The police car raced
after him. They were clearly out to get him. He drove faster than
ever before. The chase had begun.

Matigari did not know what to do. He felt like stopping the
car and running for it into the forest. But he might get caught.
Doubt and regret began eating into him. If only I had first gone

to the house. But how would I have supported my claim for what is rightfully mine with bare hands?

The police car followed closely. Matigari drove on, trying to work out the best way of shaking off the police. If only there were a side road, he could perhaps take it. But supposing it led to a dead end? He did not lose hope. He kept on looking either side of the road as he drove on. Perhaps he could do a U-turn if he came to a junction or a roundabout.

Suddenly another car appeared in front of him. It was another police car. He was trapped between two police cars. How was he ever going to escape?

The blue lights on the roofs of the police cars flashed. The police also flashed their headlights at him, signaling him to stop. The car in front of him drove on the same side of the road as he did, and the one behind him tailed closely. They were trying to sandwich him between them. They thought that they would scare him sufficiently to make him stop or drive into the ditch that ran along the road. He cautiously stepped on the brakes, applying just enough pressure to make the car slow down considerably, as though he were about to stop. The police cars slowed down too. But Matigari was only preparing himself. He made sure that there were no other cars coming from either direction.

And then suddenly he quickly made a complete U-turn and drove back the way he had come.

The police were taken by surprise, and before they could avoid it they had rammed into one another. By the time they had worked out what had happened, Matigari had traveled a fair way.

The two police cars now drove after him. How did they know that I am the one driving this car? Matigari asked himself. Could it be that the informer had phoned the police? He remembered that the minister's wife had reported that her car had been stolen. What bad luck it was that the man she had been making love with was her driver and not another man! Had it been somebody else, she wouldn't have been so quick to report that the car had been stolen. But perhaps she might have reported that whoever she was with was just a passenger. But what am I thinking? Matigari wondered. If? If? If? If? Misfortune knows no regrets. It cannot be predicted.

The police cars followed him. Matigari could see them in the rear-view mirror. But he realized that, although the police cars were faster than the one he was driving, they were avoiding driving too close to him. He understood why. They thought that he was armed. Hadn't the radio announced that the people who had stolen the car were armed? Matigari felt laughter well up in him. Then just as quickly he became very angry when he thought that the police had cut off every possible route that might lead him to the *mũgumo* tree where his weapons were.

Even so, come what may, Matigari resolved that he would not let Boy steal his future. How would he get to the tree?

Then he firmly made up his mind as to what course of action to take. The house belonged to him. Fortune favors the brave. He would follow the way of Iregi revolutionaries.

He took the road leading to the house. The police continued following him, their blue lights flashing across the evening sky as they rotated. The sirens filled the evening silence with their shrill wail.

What a surprise it was for him when he came to the road leading to the house. The whole country seemed assembled there. Cars were parked everywhere. Every single space on both sides of the road had been taken.

There were so many people. The soldiers were evident everywhere, carrying guns and torches. The security lights of the house were on, lighting up the grounds around the house in every direction. They also lit up the faces of those who stood close to the house.

Some policemen walked around with their dogs. This time they were not just the two that Matigari had come across earlier, but more, many more. It was as though the dogs too were waiting for Matigari ma Njirũũngi.

Just then the crowd spotted the Mercedes, escorted by the two police cars. Everybody thought that it was a VIP arriving.

Matigari must be somebody indeed. How feared he was, seeing that even such VIPs were coming to wait for his Second Coming, people thought.

The police driving after him were very pleased with themselves. Ah! they thought. We've got him now. They knew that the road on which Matigari drove ended up in a dead end. They slowed down confidently.

None of the people present knew what was going on.

Only Gũthera and Mũriũki did.

But even they did not know the means by which Matigari was going to arrive. How will we get him to know where we are? they wondered, as they stood among the children.

Their spirits fell when they saw Matigari behind the wheel of the Mercedes.

He was in danger, they realized, as they watched the police drive close behind. They could not figure out how Matigari could have got himself caught in such a situation, or how he was going to get himself out of it. He was surrounded on all sides.

The policemen standing at the gate opened it and saluted Matigari as he drove in. They did not know who the one in the car was. They were simply wondering: Who is this dignitary? Everybody was whispering the same question. Who was this dignitary in a black Mercedes-Benz? Yet they were not surprised at the fact that a VIP had come to the scene. They all knew how the government and the ruling party were worried about Matigari's second coming. Even if Matigari were Christ himself, he must be arrested immediately or even be shot on sight.

Matigari drove towards the garage and swung the wheel to one side. The nose of the car now pointed towards the main entrance of the house. He drove straight into the door, taking it along with him right into the building.

The police cars came to a sudden halt outside. The policemen in them came out with their guns at the ready. Gĩcerũ the informer got out with them. One carried a walkie-talkie, and he began speaking into it.

The people saw the soldiers and policemen quickly surround the house. More army lorries arrived and unloaded the Paramilitary Shooting Unit, their guns at the ready. The people suddenly understood what was going on. They all began shouting, "Matigari ma Njirũũngi! Matigari ma Njirũũngi!"

The officer in charge now stood on top of his Land-Rover and addressed the crowd with a loudspeaker.

"There is a gang of very dangerous criminals inside the house," he said. "They are armed!"

He now turned to the house and made another announcement. He had a powerful voice which reverberated in the still darkness that seemed to fill the whole world.

"Matigari, you and your followers, whoever you are, you must all surrender! You are surrounded on all sides by the security forces! *Surrender!* Come out of the house, with your hands in the air. No harm will come to you."

Outside, the crowd continued shouting:

"Matigari! Matigari!"

The officer in charge of the Paramilitary Shooting Unit warned them. Whoever dared to cheer again would be shot down there and then. A solemn silence fell over them — a silence not so much as a result of the warning, but due more to the tension arising from excitement as they waited to see what the outcome would be.

The officer in charge of the armed forces made the announcement again:

"Matigari, we know that you are in the house. Give yourself up. Surrender! Nobody will harm you. You can tell those others you are with to do the same. But if you don't surrender, you'll be shot dead. You are surrounded on all sides. You have no way of escaping. Don't listen to Matigari."

The spotlights, searchlights and torches now lit up the house from every direction. The soldiers stealthily approached the building, crouching behind trees, cars and shrubs and trying to make sure that a person inside the house could not see their movements.

"Whatever you do now, you are covered. This is a warning. I am giving you five minutes to surrender; otherwise I shall give the order to fire."

After each minute, the officer called out a warning:

"You have four more minutes left."

"Three more minutes."

"Two more minutes."

"One!"

Suddenly a ball of fire burst out of the windows of the house.

And now it was as though the people's mouths were also suddenly opened. They shouted and scrambled! The crowd surged forward towards the house. The soldiers were completely taken by surprise. They could not hold back the surging crowd.

"Boy's house is burning! Boy's house is burning!" they sang.

Some people tried to climb into the house through those windows which seemed free of smoke. They wanted to loot the house. They each wanted to ensure that they took something, however small, from the house.

"Bad Boy's house is burning! Bad Boy's house is burning!" they sang on.

Thick clouds of smoke drove back those who were trying to enter the house through the windows. Tongues of fire curled dangerously round the window frames. The crowd retreated, forming a huge ring as they did so. They continued singing:

It's burning!
Yes, Bad Boy's house is burning.
Let's warm ourselves with it.
It's burning!

They surrounded the house, singing, "Boy's property is burning!. . ."

The officer in charge called for the fire brigade with his walkie-talkie. He also asked for reinforcements, because the crowd looked as though it was getting out of control and might attack and overwhelm the security forces or start burning other houses in the vicinity.

A loud explosion was heard from the building. Bits and pieces of shattered stone were hurled up into the air, some of them falling on the crowd. It was as if the house had been blown up by a bomb.

It was the Mercedes-Benz finally exploding into flames and adding to the brightness of all the tongues of fire already spitting from the house in every direction.

The tongues all merged into one great bonfire. The flames lit up the whole compound, the fields and the surrounding country.

It was the children who started the events which followed. They shouted, "Even these other houses should burn!" They turned the call into a refrain:

Everything that belongs to these slaves must burn!
Yes, everything that belongs to these slaves must burn!
Their coffee must burn!
Yes, their coffee must burn!
Their tea must burn!
Yes, their tea must burn!

The rest of the people made more torches now from the burning house and they joined in the singing:

Their cars must burn!
Yes, their cars must burn!
Let all the other oppressors' cars burn!
Yes, let all the other oppressors' cars burn!
And those of the traitors too!
Yes, and those of the traitors too!

The property of those robbing the masses must burn!
The property of those robbing the masses must burn!
Parrotology in the land must burn!
Yes, Parrotology in the land must burn!

The culture of Parrotry must burn!
Yes, the culture of Parrotry must burn!

Nationality-chauvinism must burn!
Yes, nationality-chauvinism must burn!

Their They actually started burning all the Mercedes-Benzes that were in sight. Their owners ran for their lives. The only ones which escaped were those parked at the edges of the compound and by the main road.

The people split into groups and moved to the different houses and estates. They thus rendered the security forces helpless. They set the houses on fire.

They burned down the houses.
They burned down the tea-bushes.
They burned down the coffee-trees.
They burned down the vehicles.

And as they did this, they intensified their singing, as if they were now at war with the oppressors:

Burn detention without trial — burn!
Burn detention without trial — burn!

Burn the exiling of patriots — burn!
Burn the exiling of patriots — burn!

Burn the prisons holding our patriotic students — burn!
Burn the prisons holding our patriotic students — burn!

Burn the prisons holding all our patriots — burn!
Burn the prisons holding all our patriots — burn!

Burn Parrotology — burn!
Burn Parrotology — burn!

But above all this activity and commotion, they were all asking themselves the same question: Where was Matigari ma Njirũũngi?

The security forces were asking themselves the same: Where was Matigari ma Njirũũngi?

The officer in charge ordered the security to try to stop this wanton destruction of private property. They fired shots in the air.

When John Boy Junior heard that his house had been set on fire, he fainted. He was rushed to hospital. Where would his wife and children stay on their return from their summer holidays in the USA?

John Boy was not alone in this private terror. Many a *comprador* tycoon had a sleepless night then. They thought and claimed that the insurrection had been carefully planned. Still they wondered: Who really was this Matigari? Was this insurrection the start of another guerrilla struggle — a repeat of the struggle like the one that had been waged against colonialists? And why didn't the security forces shoot down all those carrying out this arson? How on earth could they have allowed Matigari to slip through their fingers? No! There must have been plans for a *coup d'état*, some of them concluded.

When the news of the insurrection and the acts of arson reached His Excellency Ole Excellence, he immediately promulgated a new law: Shoot on sight, shoot to kill. He then ordered that Matigari be brought to the state house *Dead Or Alive.*

Some soldiers remained at the site, waiting for the fire to die down so that they could look for Matigari's remains.

When the fire brigade came, they did not know how to begin dealing with the fire. They stood there mesmerized at the side of the road, their sirens wailing into the night.

More soldiers arrived in lorries. They rushed to protect the homes that had not yet been set alight or attacked.

It was Gĩcerũ the informer who first spotted Matigari's hat in the fields near the gate.

The officer in charge asked for the dogs. . . Two policemen leading two alsatians rushed to their boss. The dogs caught the scent.

"Bring me Matigari, dead or alive," the officer in charge ordered, echoing the wishes of His Excellency Ole Excellence. He offered a prize of £5,000 to any policeman or soldier who would bring him Matigari, dead or alive.

The greatest search that had ever been witnessed in that area began. It began even before the flames of the burning houses had subsided. But the soldiers in the hunt were worried: Who is Matigari? they asked one another. How on earth are we going to recognize him? What does he look like? What nationality is he? Is Matigari a man or woman anyway? Is he young or old? Is he fat or thin? Is he real or just a figment of people's imagination? Who or what really *is* Matigari ma Njirũũngi? Is he a person, or is it a spirit?

20

"HOW did you manage to escape?" Gũthera asked Matigari.

"I escaped through the window!" Matigari answered. His heart was heavy with sorrow. But he looked straight ahead of him, as if searching for something in the distance.

"Weren't you scared, with so many guns pointing at you?" Mũriũki asked.

"Of course I was scared," Matigari answered. "But we have to learn to fight fear. We must wage war on the fear that has descended on this land. Fear itself is the enemy of the people. It breeds misery in the land. . . But how did you find me in this crowd?"

"Your hat," Gũthera said.

"Where is it now?" Mũriũki asked.

"I don't know where it fell," Matigari answered, "but it doesn't matter. It has served its purpose; at least it led you to where I was."

"I thought that you got burned in the house," Gũthera said.

"I thought that you would get arrested by the police," Mũriũki said.

"Or get shot!" Gūthera added.

Matigari, Gūthera and Mūriūki were resting on a hill. It was dark, but Matigari knew all the paths. They headed for the *mūgumo* tree where Matigari had hidden his weapons: the AK47, the pistol, the cartridge belt and the sword. Far behind, they could still see the flames as they leaped into the sky.

"So deep a darkness is always closely followed by dawn," Gūthera said.

"Yes, it is nearly dawn," Matigari answered. "What is that song we used to sing?

If only it were dawn,
If only it were dawn,
So that I can share the cold waters with the early bird. . .
Dawn is here, and the sun has long risen —"

Before he had finished the song, they heard dogs barking.

"We are being followed," Matigari said. "But cast away your fears, be prepared, for this is only the beginning of many hardships ahead."

"Where are the dogs barking from?" Mūriūki asked.

"They are in the valley behind us," Matigari said.

They walked down the slope in silence. Behind them they could see the flickering of the policemen's torches. The torches drew closer and closer, all the time shortening the gap between them.

"If we hurry up we might get to the *mūgumo* tree before they catch up with us," Matigari said, trying to instill hope in them. "Once I wear my belt, none of them will be able to cross the river, even if they come in thousands."

The hunt lasted the whole night. Soon the horizon was painted with the first hints of dawn. Matigari, Gūthera and Mūriūki were very tired. The river was not far off now, but the dogs were closing in on them. Between where they were and the river was an open space.

"If we manage to cross the river you see over there," Matigari said, "the enemy will never be able to touch us. There in those forests and mountains we shall light the fire of our liberation. Our first independence has been sold back to imperialism by the servants they put in power!"

They suddenly realized then that they were being tracked from every direction. The pack of dogs behind them looked like a flock of sheep. Matigari remembered how Settler Williams and his friends had gone fox-hunting long ago.

"All they need now are horses to complete the picture of a hunt," Matigari said, trying to figure out how they were going to cross the stream.

"Oh, look!" Mũriũki exclaimed. "They have horses over there!"

Indeed, on their left and on their right were mounted police, accompanied by a pack of dogs. Behind them were more policemen on foot, also with dogs.

"We are the foxes," Matigari told them. "We have to run like foxes now. Don't run in a straight line. Try running from side to side. Are you ready? OK, let's go!"

They dashed into the open space and made for the stream, across which their lives awaited them.

And then suddenly the whole world was filled with the sound of gunfire.

Gũthera screamed and fell to the ground. Matigari and Mũriũki threw themselves on to the ground too, but were not hurt.

"Keep crawling! But remember, not in a straight line!" Matigari urged Mũriũki. "Mũriũki, cross the river, and bring me my AK47 from under the *mũgumo* tree. Try to do your very best to get back to me.'

Mũriũki took off. He ran in a zigzag manner. At times he fell, and rolled over, but he still got up and ran, heading in the direction of the river. He crossed it.

Gũthera was still screaming. She had been wounded in the right leg and it was bleeding profusely.

"Go! Just go!" she told Matigari. "Leave me behind. Let me die. Let me die."

But Matigari lifted her in his arms and carried her towards the river. The dogs, the soldiers and the horses drew nearer and nearer. Gunshots could be heard, ringing from all sides.

Matigari seemed to be protected by some magic power, for the bullets did not hit him. . . It was as if on reaching him they turned into water.

Before him was the river. It was so close. . . a few more steps. . . The dogs were barking just behind them.

The swishing and swirling of the water reached Matigari as it flowed by. A step more. . . and he would be swimming in it. . . Just one more. . .

The dogs leaped on Matigari and Gūthera. They crowded around them. They tore at their clothes, their flesh. But not once, not once did Matigari let go of Gūthera. Their blood mingled and it trickled into the soil, on the banks of the river.

The mounted police and soldiers came racing towards them. Even the soldiers on foot came running towards the big catch. Matigari mustered all the strength he could and, still holding Gūthera in his arms, he crawled on his knees, pulling behind him the pack of dogs that were growling as they fought for human flesh.

Matigari and Gūthera fell into the river.

Drops of water splashed into the air, wetting the dry earth by the banks of the river.

The dogs hesitated at the river banks, their tongues dangling out of their mouths. Some licked the blood on their muzzles. A few others were growling as if announcing to the world: *Sisi mbwa kali.**

And suddenly lightning flashed, and a peal of thunder rent the sky. At first a few drops of rain fell, one here, another there. Then a deluge came from the skies.

The whole army of hunters had now arrived at the water's edge. Some of the soldiers were still on horseback, others still on foot.

They were very angry, really bitter with fate; the gift of £5,000 was drifting away somewhere in the swirling river.

They walked along the river bank, hoping to see the bodies of Matigari and Gūthera floating on the water or else lying somewhere on the banks. Were they dead or alive? Who was Matigari?

The rain poured as if all the taps of heaven had been turned on full blast.

To this day, rumor has it that the torrential rain that fell was what put out the fires that had earlier consumed the houses. Across the land, children came out to sing:

---

*Sisi mbwa kali (Kiswahili): "we are fierce dogs."

Rain; Rain,
Let me slaughter you a calf,
And another
With jingle bells around the neck!

Everywhere in the country the big question still remained:
Who was Matigari ma Njirũũngi? Was he dead, or was he alive?

21

Under the *mũgumo* tree, Mũriũki dug up all the things
that Matigari had hidden.

He took out the pistol and the cartridge belt. He counted the
bullets. Then he took the AK47 and gazed at it. He dug up the
sword and laid it to one side.

He put on the cartridge belt across his chest, over his left
shoulder, so that it hung on his right side. He passed the strap of
the sword over his right shoulder and across his chest so that the
sword lay on his left side.

Finally he picked up the AK47 and slung it over his shoulder.
He stood for a while under the *mũgumo* tree.

And then he heard the sound of hoofs nearby. His heart
skipped a beat. But it was only a riderless horse. It galloped past
him. It stopped for a brief while and gazed at him. Then it disappeared into the forest.

Mũriũki watched the rain as it fell. His glance swept the banks
along which he stood. He looked across the river and beyond to
the other valleys, other ridges and other mountains.

Far, far away, he heard the distant sound of the siren as it
called out to all the workers.

He recalled the night of the workers' strike. And suddenly he
seemed to hear the workers' voices, the voices of the peasants,
the voices of the students and of other patriots of all the different
nationalities of the land, singing in harmony:

Victory shall be ours!
Victory shall be ours!
Victory shall be ours!
Victory shall be ours!